How dare the man be so presumptuous!

Louise was definitely displeased. Aldo had no right to inform her that she'd be having supper with him—when he hadn't even asked her first!

She said tartly, "Most kind of you, but if you don't mind, I prefer to go straight home. Some other time..."

He said silkily, "Oh, but I do mind, and some other time covers so many things, does it not? The hair must be washed, the kitchen floor must be scrubbed.... I don't know why you're avoiding me, Louise, but if you've developed a sudden dislike of me, do say so."

Taken aback, Louise could only reply, "I don't dislike you, Dr. van der Linden."

That assertion, she thought, had to be the understatement of the century.

Betty Neels is well-known for her romances set in the Netherlands, which is hardly suprising. She married a Dutchman and spent the first twelve years of their marriage living in Holland and working as a nurse. Today she and her husband make their home in a small ancient stone cottage in England's West Country, but they return to Holland often. She loves to explore tiny villages and tour privately owned homes there, in order to lend an air of authenticity to the background of her books.

Books by Betty Neels

HARLEQUIN ROMANCE

2787—A GIRL NAMED ROSE
2808—TWO WEEKS TO REMEMBER
2824—THE SECRET POOL
2855—STORMY SPRINGTIME
2874—OFF WITH THE OLD LOVE
2891—THE DOUBTFUL MARRIAGE
2914—A GENTLE AWAKENING
2933—THE COURSE OF TRUE LOVE
2956—WHEN TWO PATHS MEET
3004—PARADISE FOR TWO
3024—THE FATEFUL BARGAIN

Don't miss any of our special offers. Write to us at the following address for information on our newest releases.

Harlequin Reader Service
901 Fuhrmann Blvd., P.O. Box 1397, Buffalo, NY 14240
Canadian address: P.O. Box 603,
Fort Erie, Ont. L2A 5X3

No Need to
Say Goodbye

Betty Neels

Harlequin Books

TORONTO • NEW YORK • LONDON
AMSTERDAM • PARIS • SYDNEY • HAMBURG
STOCKHOLM • ATHENS • TOKYO • MILAN

Original hardcover edition published in 1989
by Mills & Boon Limited

ISBN 0-373-03036-3

Harlequin Romance first edition February 1990

CHAPTER ONE

IT SHOULD have been the quietest hour or so of the night in the hospital, when the ill and the not so ill slept, the accident centre was temporarily quiet and the busy nurses could pause for a snack meal or a cup of, tea. Tonight, as so often happened, an ambulance with its flashing lights brought the staff nurse to her feet, ready to meet the ambulanceman as he got to the doors.

'Coronary,' he told her briefly. 'In a bad way, too.'

The nurse nodded, said over her shoulder to the student nurse on duty with her, 'Get hold of Sister Payne, tell her it's a coronary, ask her to come,' and then she went out to the ambulance.

So it was that Sister Louise Payne, sitting at her desk in her office, her shoes off, a mug of tea at her elbow, and writing the beginnings of the report, put down her pen with a little sigh as the phone rang, lifted the receiver, listened with composure, said with calm, 'I'll be down at once, Nurse. Go back to Staff and help her. I'll get hold of Dr Giles,' and dug her feet into her shoes once more.

Dr Giles, the medical officer on duty, had just got to his bed; he grunted his displeasure at being roused from the brief snooze he had hoped for and, in answer to Sister Payne's firm voice telling him that she would meet him in the accident room, grunted again. She put down the receiver, knowing that despite the grumbles he would be there, and took herself off to the accident room.

Staff Nurse was glad to see her; the man was in a bad way and she hadn't had much experience of coronaries; Sister Payne took over without a fuss, and when Dr Giles arrived, trousers and sweater over his pyjamas, they worked together.

'Who is he?' asked Dr Giles, not pausing in his work.

Sister Payne didn't pause either. 'Staff?' she asked without turning round.

'The ambulance was called by someone who saw him lying in the street. A Mr Tom Cowdrie . . . They found an envelope in a coat pocket. I've not had time . . .'

'No, of course you haven't, Staff.' Sister Payne's glance flickered briefly towards Dr Giles. 'Ted, it's the MP . . . Staff, get the police, will you? Ted should you get Dr van der Linden?'

'Yes. Could Staff take over? Nurse can get the police, can't she?' He looked down at their unresponsive patient. 'No, better not—I'll stay here. Let Staff take over from you. You telephone.'

Sister Payne nodded her approval and sped to the phone, dialled a number and waited. The voice in her ear was tinged with irritation, to be expected at three o'clock in the morning, but her own remained admirably calm. She didn't waste time in apologies. 'A Mr Tom Cowdrie has just been brought in—the MP. A coronary. Dr Giles would be glad of your advice, sir.'

'Ten minutes,' said the voice in her ear, and the

line went dead.

If any one had had the leisure to look at the clock they would have noted that it was, in fact, nine minutes later when the senior medical consultant of St Nicholas's Hospital came silent-footed into the accident room. He was a massive man, well over six foot and heavily built, with fair hair already silvered and splendid good looks with a high-bridged nose, a firm mouth and blue eyes half hidden by their heavy lids. He was wearing a thin polo-necked sweater and trousers, but no one looking at him would have known that he had been wakened from a deep sleep, driven his car for the mile through London's streets which separated his house from the hospital, and still contrived to look as though he was on the point of doing an unhurried ward round.

He nodded to Dr Giles, smiled briefly at Sister Payne and bent over the patient, at the same time listening to Dr Giles's brief résumé.

He nodded his approval, while issuing his orders in a manner which allowed of no hanging around by his supporters. Whoever was on call in X-ray was to be roused, so too whoever was on night duty in the path. lab. 'And, Ted, if the police are here, give them Mr Cowdrie's address—his wife must be told. Deal with it, will you?'

Dr van der Linden had dragged off his sweater, the better to deal with his patient. 'Warn intensive care, Sister, will you? As soon as he's fit to move, we will get him up there.'

It was more than an hour later when Mr Cowdrie was borne carefully away to the intensive care unit; Sister Payne watched Dr van der Linden's broad

shoulders disappear through the door after the
trolley, listened with sympathy to Ted Giles's rueful
comment that there wasn't much point in going back
to his bed, made sure that the nurses in the accident
room were starting on the clearing up, and went
tiredly up to her office; it was very nearly time for her
early-morning round, and she still had the report to
write. Mr Cowdrie's wife had arrived, but so far
hadn't seen her husband; Dr van der Linden would
talk to her first, and then in all probability bring her
along for Sister Payne to solace with tea and
sympathy. She penned the report with the speed of
long practice, answered an urgent summons from the
women's medical ward with her usual calm, and was
just on her way back to her office, expecting to have a
quick cup of tea before commencing her rounds,
when Dr van der Linden bore down upon her with
Mrs Cowdrie beside him. Sister Payne paused,
stifling an urge to gallop briskly in the opposite
direction; it was all very well for Dr van der Linden;
he would in all probability take himself off home to a
couple of hours' sleep and a tasty breakfast cooked by
a loving wife . . .

She greeted him pleasantly and Mrs Cowdrie with
sympathy; she was a much younger woman than she
had expected, fair and fluffy and nicely made-up and
dressed with care. Surely, thought Sister Payne, she
wouldn't have stopped to do her face and dress so
carefully, knowing that her husband had just been
dragged back from death's door, and even now, for
that matter, had a foot still inside it?

Mrs Cowdrie was summing her up, too: a
handsome girl, tall and with a splendid figure, her

dark hair a little untidy. Her large brown eyes had shadows beneath them from tiredness and her straight nose shone; all the same, she had a serene beauty which Mrs Cowdrie would never achieve.

Dr van der Linden watched her from under hooded lids, his face without expression. He said blandly, 'Ah, Sister, would you be kind enough to give Mrs Cowdrie a cup of tea and arrange for a taxi to take her home presently? I have explained that she may remain here if she wishes, but she would prefer to go home.'

There were still fifteen minutes before she needed to start the morning round; Sister Payne murmured suitably and led Mrs Cowdrie away to sit in the office and drink her tea, but only after that lady had taken a fulsome farewell of Dr van der Linden.

'I really must go back home,' she explained to Sister Payne. 'I sleep very badly, you know, and this has upset me. I shall spend the day in bed.'

'Your husband is very ill . . .' began Louise carefully. 'There is a rest room here, if you care to stay?'

'Well, there is nothing I can do, is there? I have to think of my own health, Sister. Do you suppose that he will recover?'

Louise hid shock behind a calm face. 'I really don't know, Mrs Cowdrie. That is for Dr van der Linden to tell you.'

Mrs Cowdrie put down her cup and saucer. 'He's quite something, isn't he? I'll be off, thanks for the tea.' She looked round the office. 'Is this where you spend your nights? I suppose you knit or read to pass the time?'

She was quite serious; Sister Payne said quietly, 'I

do have things to do . . .' She telephoned for a taxi and escorted the lady to the hospital entrance, then turned her steps in the direction of the men's medical ward, to start her round. The intensive care unit first . . . Mr Cowdrie had a good chance of recovery, she considered. She frowned; Mrs Cowdrie had taken his sudden illness very coolly—what wife worth her salt would worry about her lack of sleep at such a time, let alone go back home until her husband had been declared safely out of danger? She met Dr van der Linden at the door, on his way out, and he paused to speak to her. They had known each other for some time now, and maintained a pleasant, rather cool relationship, each respecting the other without showing interest. They might, on occasion, hold a brief conversation about the weather or some similar impersonal topic, and at the hospital ball he would dance with her once, something he was obliged to do in common courtesy, but for the most part their talk was strictly professional, concerning the patients.

'Mr Cowdrie should do, Sister. I've left instructions with Staff Nurse. Let me know if you're not happy with anything.' He glanced at his watch. 'You will be handing over within another hour or so?'

He nodded unsmilingly, and walked rapidly away, doubtless to his bed, thought Louise enviously, and then reflected that, unlike her, he had a ward round in a few hours' time, whereas, once the house was quiet, she would be able to sleep.

She was a little late going off duty, since she had to give a lengthy report to the day sister on intensive care. The March morning, although bright, was chilly; she paused at the entrance to shiver. The streets around the hospital were already teeming with traffic and the buses would be full.

The big door swung open behind her and Dr van der Linden came to a halt beside her. 'I'll give you a lift,' he said pleasantly.

'Kind of you, sir, but I can get a bus . . .'

'Yes, I know.' He touched her arm. 'The car is over here.'

A Jaguar XJS, sleekly elegant and powerful. He ushered her into the front seat and got in beside her. 'Fourteen, Bick Street, Hoxton, isn't it?'

She wondered how he knew, but said nothing, only, 'You must be going out of your way.' And, when he didn't reply, 'This is very kind of you.'

Bick Street was almost in Islington; she supposed one would call it shabby genteel, with its facing rows of small villas, brick built and ugly and with mod. cons. which had been mod. at the turn of the century. Dr van der Linden drew up soundlessly before number fourteen, and its front door was flung open to allow three people and a dog to emerge. A girl, small and fair and pretty, a schoolgirl, fair, too, but a good deal taller and not as pretty, though still worth a second glance, and a schoolboy with sandy hair and glasses on his nose. The dog stayed with him, behind the girls; it was a smooth-coated type with a plumy tail and very large pointed ears.

There were no gardens before the houses; they crossed the pavement and peered at Louise through the car windows. The doctor obligingly opened the window and said, 'Good morning.'

Louise said, 'My sisters, Zoë and Christine, and my brother, Michael, and Dusty.'

They chorused their how do you dos, and Dusty barked a brief greeting.

'Dr van der Linden kindly gave me a lift.' Louise spoke briefly, and made to get out. Dr van der Linden got out, too, and opened her door.

'A pleasure, Sister Payne,' he said formally, then got in again and drove away with a vague wave of the hand.

The little group went into the house. 'I say, Louise, do you work for him? Aren't you lucky?' It was Zoë who spoke. 'And I spend my days at that dreary old typing school.'

Louise was in the hall, taking off her coat. 'Well, dear, it's only for another week or two, then you can get a smashing job with a film producer or stockbroker or something.' She followed the others into the kitchen. 'I don't work for him—he's a consultant. I only see him if he comes in for something urgent.'

'All the same, he drove you home . . .'

'Well, we met at the door.' Louise spoke absent-mindedly, turning over the few letters the postman had brought. 'Chris—Mike, are you ready for school? Away with you, my dears—see you at teatime. Have a good day.'

Alone with Zoë, she sat down at the kitchen table. She was too tired to eat much, but Zoë made fresh toast and another pot of tea, and sat with her for a while until it was time for her to leave the house, too.

'I'm back early this afternoon,' she said as she got her coat, 'so leave everything, Louise. You look as though you need a good sleep.'

Alone, Louise finished her toast, poured another cup of tea and opened her letters. Presently she would wash her dishes—the others had already done theirs—let Dusty out into the strip of garden behind the house, have a bath and go to bed. For two years now, ever since their mother's death, when she had taken over the reins of the household, they had kept to a routine which on the whole worked very well. The three younger children kept the house tidy, made their beds and laid tables and washed up, and, on her nights off duty each week, she cleaned the little house, did the week's shopping and saw to the washing and as much of the ironing as possible. It left little time for leisure, but at least they were together and had a home. There was no money, of course; just sufficient to live decently, and tucked away in the bank was the small capital her father had left, enough to send Mike to university when the time came.

They were lucky to have a home, however shabby, she reflected, unfolding the first of her letters.

It was typewritten, from their landlord, who had rented them the house when her father had had to go into hospital and her mother, knowing that his illness was terminal, had moved to London, lock, stock and barrel, not to mention her four children, so that they might be near him. When he had died they had stayed on because Louise was half-way through her training, and her mother, with some help from her, could just about manage to make ends meet. When her mother had died, two years previously, they had stayed on; Louise had a safe job, Zoë would soon be working and helping out with the housekeeping and the younger ones were doing well at school, although Louise wasn't too happy about the schools. Sensibly, she didn't allow herself to worry about the future. It was important to get the two younger ones through their exams; only then would she decide what was best to be done. It was obvious to her that, even if she met a man she would like to marry, he would jib at having to provide for her brother and sisters and, whereas while she had been training and her mother was still alive, she had never lacked for invitations from the housemen at the hospital, they had cooled off when they had discovered later that she now had responsibility for the upbringing of the family. She didn't blame them, and if she repined she did it in private, turning a calm face to the world.

Unfolding the letter, she allowed herself speculation as to its contents. Another rise in the rent, she supposed; there had never been an agreement. Years ago, when they had first moved there, there had been what the landlord had called a 'gentlemen's agreement,' and when on her mother's death she had asked him about it, he had assured her that since this arrangement had been in force for some time there was no point in altering it. She had agreed with him, and hadn't even had a rent book.

A great pity that she had agreed, she reflected, reading his letter. The house had been sold and the new owner would like to take possession as soon as possible, and since there was no written agreement and no lease to expire he would be glad if she could arrange to leave as soon as she had found suitable accommodation. The letter ended with a brief apology—the price he had been offered for the house was too advantageous to be ignored, and he regretted any inconvenience it might cause her.

She read the letter through again once more, slowly, in case she had missed something. She hadn't—there it was in black and white. She got up, cleared the table, washed the china, set the table ready for their evening meal, let Dusty in from the garden and went upstairs to run the bath, all the while her tired brain doing its best to wrestle with the news. She could get advice, she supposed, but she was pretty sure that the landlord had the law on his side; it was quite true, there was no agreement as such, and for all she knew when her mother had rented the house she might have agreed verbally to leave if asked to do so. Bick Street hadn't been much sought after; it was only in the last year or so that house prices had soared.

She got into bed and, because she was so very tired, fell asleep at once, to wake in the early afternoon and start worrying again. She had no intention of saying anything to the others, not until she had made quite sure that the landlord was within his rights and, if he was, and she was pretty sure that he was, she had done some house-hunting. She had strong doubts about being able to rent a house and, even if she could get a council flat, what would happen to Dusty?

She got up, made herself some tea and went into the tiny strip of garden with the dog. The daffodil bulbs were showing and there were late snowdrops in one corner and crocuses as well. She remembered the pleasant garden surrounding the house in the country where she had been born and brought up until her father's illness, and she sighed, but she had common sense; thinking about the past wasn't going to help the future. She went indoors and started to get the high tea they all shared, and when they were all sitting round the table, discussing the day, she joined in cheerfully and just as usual, making sure that the evening routine

of dog-walking, homework and small household chores
was in train before she took herself off to work.

It was a busy night with emergency intakes,
unexpected crises on the wards and the intensive care
unit full up. Mr Cowdrie had improved; Louise, going
along to see him, met Dr van der Linden bent on the
same errand.

He stopped abruptly, his massive proportions pre-
venting her from sidling around him with a murmured,
'Good evening, sir.'

'No sleep?' he enquired, and, at her surprised look,
'No colour, puffy lids, shadowed eyes. Something
worrying you?'

For a brief moment she toyed with the idea of flinging
herself at him and pouring out her problem; he would
be a good, patient listener, utterly impersonal and
probably able to give her sound advice for that very
reason, for he had no interest in her as a person, only as
Night Sister. The next second she said in her calm way,
'No, sir. I didn't sleep as well as usual, that's all.'

He nodded, stood aside for her to go in and followed
her to the first of the patients, and presently Ted Giles
joined them.

There were two more nights before she would be free
with nights off, and she wisely decided to do nothing
until she could occupy the whole of her mind with her
personal worries. She went about her duties in her
usual calm fashion and, although she slept badly, her
excuse to her sisters and brother that she had a cold was
accepted without suspicion.

She left the hospital later than usual after her last
night of duty; Sister Berry, who would take over from
her for three nights, had only recently been made a

sister and, although a good nurse, needed a good deal of bolstering up. Louise took care that the staff nurses on duty with her were experienced but all the same she always wrote a rather more detailed report for her.

Dr van der Linden was coming in as she was going out. His 'good morning' was preoccupied, but he paused after he had passed her and retraced his steps. 'Nights off? You look as though you need them.'

He had gone again before she could say anything; she made her way home, feeling plain and alarmingly desirous of bursting into tears.

In the afternoon, after she had had a nap and done the shopping, she went along to the two estate agents in the neighbourhood. Evidently neither of them had anything to offer her; indeed, they looked at her askance. No one rented a house these days, not when mortgages were so easy to get. There was one flat, two bedroomed, and excluding rates the rent was rather more than the sum she earned in a week. She went back home, prepared the evening meal and when they had all finished it, cleared the table and told them about the landlord's letter. 'I'm not sure what we can do,' she finished matter-of-factly, 'but since I pay the rent a month in advance and I've only just paid it, we have got more than three weeks . . .'

'Haven't we any relations?' asked Mike.

'Only Great-Aunt Letitia, but she washed her hands of Father when he married Mother. Don't worry, I'll think of something.' Louise spoke with such certainty that their relief was evident.

There was not time to talk about it in the morning; she saw them off, washed up, took Dusty for a brisk walk round the dull streets and came back to find that the postman had been. Only one letter, and that sufficiently official-looking for her to hesitate before she opened it.

She slit the envelope deliberately; there could be no worse news than that which she had had from the landlord. It might even be better . . .

It was. The letter, brief and businesslike, sent from Ridgely, Ridgely, Smith and Ridgley, Solicitors, with an address in the city, informed her that Miss Letitia Payne, her father's aunt, whom she could barely remember, had recently died and had left her house at Much Hadham and her estate, less an annuity to her housekeeper, to her eldest great-niece, Louise Payne. If Miss Payne would have the goodness to call at the above address, matters would be made clear to her.

Louise read the letter again, slowly this time, not quite believing it; she had never doubted that miracles did happen, but she hadn't expected one to happen to her. She read the letter again and then, being a practical person, got her coat and her purse and went across the street to the corner shop where there was a telephone box.

In answer to her request to speak to Mr Ridgely, a vinegary voice asked which one.

'Well, I don't suppose it matters, if you could just say that it is Miss Louise Payne.'

From the dry-as-dust voice which came on the line, she supposed that she was speaking to the most senior of the Mr Ridgelys. It sounded a little shaky, but assured her that the contents of the letter were, in fact, true. 'Solicitors, young lady, are not given to levity,' said the voice peevishly.

'So sorry,' said Louise, 'but it is a surprise. Shall I

come and see you today?'

'By all means. I shall place your affairs in the hands of Mr Gerald Ridgely, who will apprise you of all the details. If you could make it convenient to see him at noon, today?'

She got there with a few minutes to spare; there had been time for her to change into the suit she had bought at Country Casuals' sale; it wasn't quite warm enough for the chilly March day, but she felt well dressed in it. Her abundant hair she had pinned neatly into a chignon, and her shoes were well polished. After all, it was a momentous occasion, worthy of her best efforts.

The solicitors had rooms in an old house just off Holborn; steep stairs led her to the first floor, where she found a vinegar-faced and very thin woman at a desk. Upon hearing her name, the woman led her wordlessly to a door at the end of a short passage.

The man who rose to shake her hand was grey-haired and looked as though he needed a thorough dusting. 'Young Mr Ridgely,' intoned the thin woman and left them. Louise took the chair she was offered, wondering just how old the elder Mr Ridgely might be if this was the young one, and dismissed the thought as frivolous.

'You are Miss Louise Payne?' The dusty gentleman sounded suspicious. She opened her bag and produced her birth certificate, thankful that she had had the wit to bring it with her. He read it carefully and slowly, and nodded several times, and then opened the file in front of him.

'You know of your great-aunt's house and where it is situated?'

'Oh, yes. Although I haven't been there for a very long time. My parents took us there several times when they were alive.' Just in case he was still suspicious, she added, 'A small white house on a corner with trees around it.'

'Just so, Miss Payne. There are of course some changes in Much Hadham; it is a much sought-after area in which to live, being near enough to London for those who work here to commute. You could get a very good price for the house . . .'

Louise shook her head. 'I haven't had a chance to talk it over with my sisters and brother, but I think they will want to live there—I know I do.'

He looked at her over his old-fashioned, gold-rimmed spectacles. 'I understand that you are a night sister at St Nicholas's Hospital? You will be able to continue your work there if you should decide to live in your great-aunt's house?'

'Oh, no. I would have to find another job—Bishop's Stortford or Stevenage, I suppose, but it would be marvellous for Christine and Michael; they're still both at school and not very happy where they are now. Zoë, who is nearly nineteen, is just finishing a secretarial course and, I hope, will get a job.'

'There is very little money in your great-aunt's estate; she has made provision for her housekeeper,' he glanced at the files, 'Miss Wills, who is already in receipt of her retirement pension.' He coughed drily. 'The sum of one thousand, four hundred and twenty-three pounds, eighty-five pence is available to you; such debts, funeral expenses and so forth have already been discharged.'

Louise, with a bank balance of slightly less than a thousand pence, managed to restrain her yelp of delight. She asked, she hoped not too eagerly, 'Is the house furnished?'

'Yes. I should add that when I was last there, a good deal of it was too large for the house; mid-Victorian. Do you have your own furniture?'

'Well, yes, not a great deal, but what there is is rather nice—left from the house where we lived before we came to London.'

'Then if I might advise you, Miss Payne, I should visit your great-aunt's house—your house, I should say! It is called Ivy Cottage, by the way—and decide what you wish to keep; the rest you might sell and add to your capital. The money due to you will be paid into your bank if you will be so good as to let me have particulars of that before you go. The house is empty and I will give you the keys now.'

He handed over a bunch of old-fashioned keys, each one labelled. 'If there is anything I can do for you, do not hesitate to let me know. Now, if I might have the name of your bank?'

They parted soberly, because young Mr Ridgely would have been shocked if she had hugged him or danced a jig of pure joy on his Turkish carpet. She walked away from the sombre building with her feet upon air, her head full of a hundred and one ideas, most of them highly impractical. It was an occasion for champagne, singing and dancing, none of which would go down well in High Holborn. A bus home, she decided, allowing the sensible side of her nature to get the upper hand, a strong cup of tea and a good think.

Here fate took a hand: Dr van der Linden, going about his own business on the opposite side of the street, caught sight of her and, even at that distance, he could see the glow of sheer happiness on her face.

Intrigued, he crossed over.

'Either you have won the pools or you have accepted an offer of marriage from a millionaire,' he observed, not bothering with a good morning.

Louise raised her lovely eyes to his. She was in such a state that it seemed perfectly natural that he should join her there on the pavement; rather like a dream, when the most extraordinary things seemed quite normal.

'I don't know any millionaires, and I can't afford the pools, but yes, something quite marvellous has happened.'

'In that case, come and tell me all about it.'

He didn't wait for her to answer, but took her arm and walked up Grays Inn Road and turned into Theobald's Road, where he ushered her into a smart brasserie.

As they went inside, Louise said half-heartedly, 'But I must get home.'

'Of course, but you may as well lunch with me now we are here.'

It was not yet one o'clock; they had a table for two by the window and Dr van der Linden said, 'Whatever it is, you are in no state to order a meal. Allow me?'

She would have eaten dry bread and water quite cheerfully; as it was, she polished off salmon mousse, a cheese soufflé of incredible lightness and fresh pineapple doused in kirsch and whipped cream, all the while only half listening to her companion's easy flow of small talk. It was only when the coffee-tray had been set before them that he said, 'Now, supposing you unburden yourself; it won't seem real until you do.'

She still felt as though she were in a dream, which was perhaps why she began without preamble. 'I've inherited a house—from a great-aunt I haven't seen in years. The marvellous thing is this, our landlord actually gave us notice to move out of our house because it's been sold, and I had no idea what I could do.' She poured their coffee, beaming at him across the little table. 'Now we can go to Much Hadham . . .'

He interrupted her abruptly. 'Much Hadham? The village near Ware?'

She was still too bemused to notice the abruptness. 'Yes. It's a small house called Ivy Cottage. There's a garden, a real one, not just a dusty strip of grass, and trees, and Mike and Christine can go to decent schools and Zoë is bound to get a good job . . .'

'And you?' he prompted.

'Me? No, I mean I, don't I? I'll get a job at Bishop's Stortford or Stevenage.' Her practical mind was beginning to take over again. 'I'm sorry to bore you with all this; you've been very kind. I think I was so bowled over that I could have danced a jig in the middle of Holborn. You see, it's a miracle . . .'

His voice was reassuringly matter of fact. 'They do occur.'

He gave her an abstracted smile and she said hurriedly, 'Thank you for my lunch, I did enjoy it. I must be getting back.'

He made no effort to detain her, but paid the bill and walked back the way they had come. In High Holborn she stopped. 'There is my bus stop . . .'

He ignored her, and lifted an arm to a passing taxi, put her inside, closed the door on her with a suave, 'Allow me,' and paid the driver and gave her address. She sat there, too astonished to speak, while the cab bore her homewards. He hadn't even said goodbye, she remembered; he must have been bored out of his mind. She went a bright pink at the idea and the cabby, glancing back in his mirror, thought what a very pretty girl she was.

Dusty was delighted to see her again and, since there was no one else to talk to, she told him all about it while she hoovered and polished and hung out lines of washing, impatient for the others to come home.

She had tea ready for them, and over that meal told them the news.

'We would have had to move anyway,' she finished, 'but now we will have a real home of our own and no rent to pay . . .'

They sat and stared at her, speechless until Mike let out a whoop of delight. 'I'll be able to leave this school . . .'

'So will I,' crowed Christine. Not a demonstrative family by nature, they hugged each other, talking a good deal of nonsense and making outrageous plans. Louise went to the dark little pantry and fetched out a bottle of sherry she had been saving for Zoë's nineteenth birthday and opened it, and they sat round, the washing up forgotten, while she told them her own sensible plans. They agreed to everything that she suggested; she was the eldest and a good deal older than they were, and they had become accustomed to go to her for help and advice. If she said that it was the best thing for them to move, then move they would, and be overjoyed to do it.

On her first morning after her return to night duty, she went to the office and handed in her resignation; she had always got on well with the senior nursing officer, and now she was listened to with sympathy.

'In the circumstances,' declared Miss Pritchard, 'I can understand that you have no choice but to move to this house which you have been left—most fortuitously, I must add. I shall be very sorry to lose you, Sister, and can but hope that you will be able to find another post near your new home. You can rely upon me to give you an excellent reference, and if I can help in any way, I shall be glad to do so.'

Her friends at the hospital received her news with mixed feelings; she was well liked and, moreover, they had all known each other for a number of years, but they echoed Miss Pritchard's opinion; there was nothing else for Louise to do. There was no question of selling the house at Much Hadham, she would never get sufficient for it to buy anything similar in London, and in a way, she reflected on her journey home, it was nice not having to make up her mind about it; circumstances had done that for her. She composed a letter to the landlord before she went to bed, and slept soundly for the first time in days.

CHAPTER TWO

ON THE first day of Louise's next nights off they all went to Much Hadham, Dusty, on his best behaviour, going with them. It was a short journey and they were there before ten o'clock, walking down the village street with its charming mixture of sixteenth and seventeenth-century cottages and large Georgian town houses. The house was more or less in the centre of the village, standing cornerwise on to the junction of a side lane and the main street. It wasn't large but, even so, bigger than their house in Hoxton, and there was, as far as they could see as they approached it, a sizeable garden. Louise unlocked the front door and they crowded in silently, to stand in the narrow hall and gaze around them. The passage ran from the front door to the back, where there was another stout door, and on either side there were two doors, with a pretty little staircase near the back door.

After a few moments Louise walked to the back door and opened it. The garden was nicely old-fashioned, although neglected, but there was a fair-sized grass plot, flowerbeds and, along the end wall, what had been a vegetable patch with the garden shed at one end of it. Still silently she led the others into the first room: the kitchen, with a stone-flagged floor, a very elderly Aga cooker, an old-fashioned dresser and Windsor chairs around a wooden table. Its windows overlooked the garden at the back.

Louise said at once, 'Someone to see to the stove; we can paint the walls and plan to make curtains and polish the furniture . . .' She didn't wait for an answer, but led the way across the hall and opened another door. A small room with worn lino on its floor and faded curtains, but the desk in it was a charming one of rosewood, badly in need of a polish, with a sabre-legged Regency chair drawn up to it, and there was a library table against one wall, flanked by two matching chairs.

'Nice,' commented Louise, and led her party back into the hall and into the room facing the small front garden. It must have been the drawing-room, they decided, for there were several easy chairs, shabby but whole, a long case clock and a glass-fronted bookcase, as well as a pier table under the window. The carpet under their feet was faded but still good, if somewhat grubby. 'A good scrub,' said Louise as they went into the last room. The dining-room, small and rather dark by reason of the gloomy wallpaper and heavy serge curtains. But the table at its centre was solid mahogany, as were the four chairs around it, and there was a sideboard of the same wood.

They looked at each other and smiled happily and went up the stairs.

The bathroom was almost a museum piece with a bath on claw feet in the centre of the bare floor, but the geyser above it looked modern enough. The washbasin was large and, like the bath, white, with brass taps and a wooden cupboard beneath it concealing a multitude of pipes. There was lino on the floor here, too, badly in need of replacement.

There were three bedrooms, one large enough for Zoë and Christine, and two smaller ones for Mike and Louise, and at the back of the landing a tiny curved staircase leading to an attic with windows back and front.

Louise caught Mike's look. 'Once we are in and things have got sorted out, we might turn this into a room for you, Mike; that would give us a spare room. What do you all think of it? Will you be happy here?'

Their chorus of delight almost deafened her.

'We'll go and find somewhere where we can have coffee. Then, Mike, will you check the lights? Zoë and Christine, you have got the tape measure? We shall need curtains everywhere; I'm going to see if I can get hold of someone to look at that Aga, and we'll have to have the floors done. But first we must clean up the place and polish the furniture; we can use most of it except that big bed upstairs. I think there will be enough money to get emulsion and do the painting—if we all come here on my next nights off, we should be able to get a good deal done. We'll have to picnic.' She frowned. 'I might be able to find someone in the village who would give us bed and breakfast . . .'

A question solved for her, for, when they got back after having coffee, Miss Wills knocked briskly on the door, introduced herself and suggested without preamble that they might be glad of her help.

'You intend to live here? I thought that you might; it is a dear little house, and so convenient. If you will allow me, I will point out what needs to be done.'

Which she did, at the same time giving the names and addresses of those who might undertake the various repairs. Her sharp eyes swept over the little group surrounding her. 'I expect you will do your own painting and cleaning?'

Louise nodded. 'Oh, yes. We haven't much money, but I can see that there are some repairs which must be done before we can move in. I can't leave my job for another three weeks, although I can come down for my nights off.'

Miss Wills coughed. 'I have retired, as you must know; my sister and I share a house in the village. We do bed and breakfast, but at this time of the year we have rooms to spare. You are all welcome to have beds and breakfasts at a nominal sum.'

Louise gazed at the elderly lady facing her; she had spoken briskly and her severe features had relaxed only slightly, but Louise sensed that she was being friendly and sincere. She said, 'That is very kind of you, Miss Wills. I haven't got things worked out yet, but I think that we might all come down on my next nights off and get the house cleaned and begin the painting. Do you suppose that it would be too soon if I were to come back tomorrow and see about carpets and the Aga? If the floors are done, it will be so much easier to move the furniture around and bring down what we have in Hoxton.'

'I don't see why not. You need Mr Baxter for the Aga and Ted Poolley for the floors—you'll need to do the cleaning and painting first before he comes, of course, but you could discuss what you need and get an estimate.'

So matters were arranged, and Miss Wills took herself off with a further recommendation to Louise to let her know if she needed a bed at any time.

'Well, I must say,' declared Louise when she had gone, 'it's as though our fairy godmother has turned up at last.'

It seemed as if she were right. Mr Baxter, when she saw him the next day, undertook to deal with the Aga, put new washers on all the taps and give the plumbing what he called the 'once over', and Ted Poolley, a tall, spidery man who had almost nothing to say, agreed to measure up the kitchen and bathroom floors for a good hardwearing covering and left a book of samples for carpeting. Louise wasn't sure if there would be enough money for that and she said so, whereupon he advised her to put an advertisement in Mrs Potter's newspaper shop window, and sell anything she didn't want in the house. She thanked him, went round the place with pencil and paper and found that there were quite a few tables and chairs, as well as the bed, which she didn't need. She wrote out her advertisement before she did anything else, and took it with her when she went to buy Harpic, liquid soap and a strong disinfectant. She bore these back with her and began a vigorous cleaning session, draped in an old apron she had found hanging in the kitchen. She paused for sandwiches and a pot of tea in the middle of the day and, satisfied with the cleanliness of the kitchen, started on the bedroom. She was on her knees poking under the cupboard when she heard footsteps in the hall below. Someone come to inspect the furniture she hoped to sell? She got to her feet, just in time to see Dr van der Linden open the door wide and come in.

She stood, a deplorable sight in her old apron, her hair tied back anyhow, her face shining with her efforts, her hands and arms wrinkled from hot soapsuds, and she gaped at him. 'Whatever are you doing here?' She added a 'sir' hastily, and closed her mouth with something of a snap.

'I happened to be passing; I'll give you a lift back.'

'But I'm not ready, it's only three o'clock—I mean to catch the train that leaves just after five. It's very kind of you . . .'

'I don't intend to leave until five o'clock in any case.' He smiled at her, and she wondered why he looked so amused.

'Oh, you've a patient here?'

'No—at least, not one that I need to visit. I live here.'

Her pretty mouth dropped open once more. 'Live here? Do you? In Much Hadham?'

He came right into the room and sat down on a chair. 'Yes. In the High Street.' He named one of the large eighteenth-century houses, dignified bow-windowed residences with splendid doorways, opening straight on to the street, but with large walled gardens at their backs.

'Well, I never,' observed Louise rather inadequately. 'I thought you lived somewhere in London.' She blushed as she spoke, because it sounded as though she took an interest in his private life.

He watched the blush with pleasure. 'I have a flat there, but I do my best to spend as much time as possible here.' He stretched his long legs comfortably. 'Don't let me interrupt your work. When do you move?'

'Oh, in a week or two; there's quite a lot to be done first, and we can stay in Hoxton until the month's notice is up.' She began to wash the paintwork of the cupboard; it was all very well for her visitor to take his ease; she needed every minute of her free time if the house was to be fit to move into.

'Have you found another job?' he wanted to know.

She gave the cupboard a final wipe, and sat back on

her heels to admire her handiwork. 'Well, I haven't had much time,' she pointed out reasonably. 'I thought I'd try Stevenage; it's a pretty big place, and there's a lot of industry there and probably the hospital could do with more staff . . .'

'But perhaps not a sister's post—will you settle for day duty?'

He spoke idly and she answered him with unthinking frankness. 'Oh, lord, yes. I'm not going to be fussy. I shan't have any rent to pay here; you have no idea what a fantastic difference that will make; so I can take anything I'm offered. I'd rather have a ward, of course, but I'm not out for promotion; this——' she waved a soapy arm around her '—is quite the most wonderful thing that has happened to us for ages . . . for a long time.'

'Since your parents died?' said Dr van der Linden softly.

She scrubbed a windowsill with vigour; her quite wretched tongue, running away with her like that. She said 'yes', shortly and added, 'It's a lovely day . . .'

The doctor's eyes gleamed with amusement. 'Indeed it is. Do you know anyone living here?'

'No——Well, Miss Wills, who kept house for my great-aunt, she called yesterday and was very helpful—about plumbers and all that.'

'A nice old lady—very respected in the village. There are some good schools round and about, but I expect you know that.'

'No, I didn't, but I hoped there would be.' Louise put up a wet hand and swept back a lock of dark hair. 'State or private?'

'Both. Possibly your brother and sister might get

scholarships. Are they happy where they are at present?'

She was polishing a small toilet mirror on the chest of drawers; it was apple wood, not valuable but nicely made with a well-fitting drawer beneath it; with the dust washed off it, it was quite charming. 'They hate it,' she told him.

'And you? You have hated living in Hoxton?'

She nodded. 'It's been worse for Zoë—she's young and so pretty, and she has had no fun.'

He gave her a thoughtful look; he could only see her profile. She had a determined chin; probably she was an obstinate girl, and proud.

'Very pretty,' he agreed blandly. 'I have no doubt that she will find a job and friends without any difficulty. How long are you going to kneel there, scrubbing?'

'Until five o'clock, Dr van der Linden.' Something in her voice implied that it was time that they got back to their usual relationship of cool, friendly respect.

He ignored it. 'You don't mind if I call you Louise? After all, you are not on duty now.' He didn't wait for her to answer, but got to his feet and strolled to the door. 'I'll be back here at five o'clock; we'll have tea and I will drive you back home.'

He had gone while she was still trying to find a good reason for not accepting his invitation.

'Well,' said Louise indignantly, addressing the empty room, 'it was more of an order.' She frowned. 'And I talked too much. Whatever came over me?'

She attacked the bedside table with unnecessary force; it was an ordinary white-painted piece of furniture, like the bed, but when the room was carpeted and curtained and there were flowers and ornaments around it would do very well. She worked with a will; by five to five she was finished and had tidied away the bucket and brush, washed out the apron, combed her hair and done something to her face. Her hands were still red, but at least they were clean and she had nice nails, well kept and a good shape. She was locking the back door when Dr van der Linden opened the front door and walked in.

'Punctual,' he commented pleasantly. 'You bring your disciplined working life into your private living. Very commendable.'

A remark to which for some reason Louise took exception.

At the back of her head had been the vague idea that he would take her to his house for tea, but she was wrong. He ushered her into the car and drove off through the village, and, when they reached Stanstead Abbots, stopped at Briggens House and ushered her inside its elegant portals and ordered tea and delicate little sandwiches and mouth-watering cakes. She enjoyed it all; all the same she felt disappointment at not going to his house—after all, it was so close to Ivy Cottage. Perhaps his wife was there—but was he married? She had never bothered about his private life before and there was no point in starting now, she reminded herself smartly, carrying on the kind of conversation she was in the habit of having with the consultant at the hospital when they stopped to chat upon occasion.

Dr van der Linden watched her face unobtrusively, reading her thoughts very accurately, while bearing his part in their talk with the cool pleasantness he exhibited when they met at hospital, so that her uneasiness sub- sided; he was, after all, only doing what any charitable- minded person would do for someone they knew, however slightly.

Bick Street, despite the neatness of its little houses, was a different kettle of fish from Much Hadham. Louise reflected that she wouldn't feel a spark of regret when they left it. She voiced her thoughts as the doctor stopped before her front door. 'I shall be glad to leave here,' she said, and turned to thank him for her lift. But Zoë had opened the door and was already standing by the car, her pretty, eager face beaming at them.

'I've just made tea; come and have a cup with us Dr van der Linden?'

Louise began, 'Oh, but we've . . .'

But she was forestalled by his calm, 'That would be delightful,' and his speedy removal of his vast person from his car. He came and opened the door for her, smiling down at her so that she found it quite impossible to say anything more.

Inside the house they went into the sitting-room, where signs of their departure were much in evidence, with packing cases in corners and books piled tidily. The tea-tray was on a corner of the table by the window, and Zoë said, 'There is plenty in the pot . . .' and raised her voice to call, Christine, bring that cake Louise made yesterday, and find Mike; tea is made.' She smiled at Louise. 'I'll pour, Louise, you look tired. How come you met Dr van der Linden?'

'He lives at Much Hadham . . .'

Christine and Mike had joined them. The three younger members of the family turned surprised faces to their guest and chorused happily, 'How utterly super—do you live near Ivy Cottage? Are you married? Did you know Great-Aunt Payne?'

Louise's quiet voice brought them all to a halt. 'My

dears, I hardly think that Dr van der Linden would wish to answer you.'

Zoë said at once, 'Oh, sorry, we didn't mean to be rude. It was awfully kind of you to bring Louise back, though; it's saved her hours. Have some of this cake; she is a marvellous cook.'

Louise was astonished to see him eat a slice with evident appetite, after the splendid tea they had had, too. Of course, he was a very large man; moreover he was kind; he was probably eating it for fear of hurting her feelings. The conversation centred round the trials of moving house, enlivened by Dusty's antics and Mike's high-flown ideas as to what he intended to do with the attic at Ivy Cottage. The doctor sat back at his ease, listening with interest and occasionally putting in a question. It was almost an hour before he rose, saying that he had an appointment and would have to go. Louise thanked him again politely as he took his leave, but it was Zoë who went out to the car with him, and stood talking by it for a few more minutes.

Louise, glancing out of the window, frowned thoughtfuly. Dr van der Linden and Zoë seemed taken with each other, but her sister was very young, he must be almost twice her age. Besides, he hadn't answered their questions, had he? She supposed that she could find out easily enough at the hospital if he was married or not, but that was something she would never do. In any case, she told herself they were very unlikely to see much of him; once they had moved the two youngest would be at school, Zoë would get a job and she would, with luck, have a job in Stevenage. With Zoë earning as well as herself, and no rent to pay, there would be more money; Zoë would be able to have some pretty clothes and join a tennis club, get to know young people of her own age. Louise, her thoughts busy with the future, turned away from the window and went along to the kitchen to see what there was for supper.

She made the journey to Ivy Cottage again the next day; she was on duty that night, but it was worth going for the morning at any rate; she was sure she would have time to clean out another bedroom, and perhaps someone would come and buy the bed.

Her hopes were realised; the bedroom was a small room and there wasn't much furniture in it. She had washed the paint and cleaned the walls ready for the painting they would do the next time they came, and was consulting with Mr Baxter about the Aga, when an elderly couple thumped the knocker.

They had a daughter getting married, they explained, and the bed might do as a wedding present. Louise led them upstairs and watched patiently while they tried the springs, examined the mattress and, finally, offered her rather less than she had asked. She accepted without demur; the money would come in very handy, and the bed would be out of the way. They had a van outside; the bed was dismantled and stowed safely, and both parties parted on the best of terms, well satisfied. If the tables and chairs were sold as easily there would be money enough to have the kitchen modernised a little: she went straight back to Mr Baxter and sounded him out upon the matter. He had just the thing, he assured her, some cupboards and shelves someone had ordered and then cancelled at the last minute. Going cheap; he mentioned a price well within her budget and she sighed with relief; something on the floor and some curtains at the window, and at least one room in the little house would be ready for use.

She had time for a brief nap before she went on duty, and when Dr van der Linden encountered her as he left the women's medical ward, she looked her usual self, unshakeably calm and as neat as a new pin. His 'Good evening, Sister,' was uttered with impersonal politeness before he went on to discuss with her the condition of one of his patients; that he had sat and watched her cleaning furniture in an old apron and with her hair anyhow, smacked of the nonsensical, and from his manner it seemed plain to her that he had dismissed it from his mind. And why not? common sense demanded of her, while at the same time she felt a decided peevishness at his lack of friendliness.

She didn't see him again until she was on the point of leaving the hospital five days later, with the prospect of two nights off duty, her head full of plans as to what to do first at Ivy Cottage. The last of these days fell, most fortunately, on a Saturday, which meant that all four of them would be able to work there. The sitting-room, she decided, as she changed out of her uniform; if they could do the walls and paintwork, then the carpets could be laid, and in the meantime she could start on the dining-room. They would have to move out of the house in Bick Street in less than a week's time . . . She started downstairs on her way out, deep in thought.

Dr van der Linden followed her silent-footed, caught up with her on the first landing, and asked, 'Nights off? Do you plan to go to Much Hadham today? I shall be driving there this morning. Can I give you a lift? Around ten o'clock?'

She had stopped to look at him, tired eyes from her beautiful face searching his own blue eyes, half hidden under their heavy lids.

'Thank you,' she said at length. 'I did intend going there today, and I'd be grateful.'

'Good.' He spoke briskly. 'I will be outside your place; if there is anything to take down there, it can go in the boot.'

Too good an opportunity to miss; Louise had a number of cardboard boxes and plastic bags tidily lined up in the little hall by the time the doctor arrived. She had seen Mike and Christine off to school, eaten a hasty breakfast with Zoë, attended to Dusty's wants, and had a shower, so that when she opened the door to him she appeared ready for a day's work at the cottage. He gave her a searching glance, accepted the coffee she offered, fended off Dusty's pleased advances, and sat down for all the world as though he had the morning to waste. Louise, in a fever to get on with the manifold jobs awaiting her, and aware that if she sat still for any length of time she would fall asleep, drank her own coffee so fast that she scalded her tongue, and then sat watching him take his time over his own drink. When they were at last in the car with her boxes and bags stowed and Dusty, to his delight, on the back seat—for as Dr van der Linden had pointed out he might just as well spend the day at Ivy Cottage since they would be returning at around five o'clock and could be conveyed without trouble—he observed casually that he for his part had not the least objection to her closing her eyes and taking a refreshing nap.

'Thank you,' said Louise frostily, still nettled at his tardiness, 'I am not in the least sleepy.' And, within seconds of saying it, had nodded off.

At Ivy Cottage he wakened her gently, took the door

key from her and went to open the front door. He
deposited her bundles in the hall and led Dusty to the
safety of the little back garden. Which gave her time to
become thoroughly awake. As he ushered her from the
car, he remarked in his calm way, 'It is not of the least
use advising you to get on to the nearest bed and sleep,
although that is what you need more than anything else.
Fortunately you are a well-built girl with plenty of
stamina, even if you are of a managing disposition. I see
Mr Baxter is already at work, and Ted Poolley is on his
knees measuring the stairs. I have put Dusty in the
garden.'

'You have been very kind. I am sorry I was snappy, it's
just that there is so much to do . . .'

'And that reminds me,' interpolated the doctor, 'my
gardener's grandson is staying with him—a lad of fifteen
or so; he has been helping around the garden, but there
is very little for him to do there at the moment and he is
at a loose end. You would be rendering me a service by
taking him off his grandfather's hands for an hour or so.
Don't pay him—he has had his week's wages in advance
. . . His name is Tim.'

'But I must pay him . . .'

'You shall settle up later; don't complicate things at
present. He's a handy lad; give him some painting to
do.'

The doctor nodded briefly, and had taken himself off
before she could argue the matter, and five minutes later
a tall, skinny youth presented himself at the door. He
grinned shyly.

'Tim, miss, come to give you a hand.'

Louise was no longer tired; a great part of the day was
before her, Mr Baxter was putting up shelves with the

speed of light, Mr Poolley was in the dining-room now, with his ruler and notebook, and here was willing help. She beamed at Tim. 'Can you paint?' she asked happily.

Even with a coffee break, the four of them had got through a prodigious amount of work by one o'clock: the shelves were up, the cupboards were in position, the Aga worked and she had decided on the carpeting with Ted Poolley. It would make a big hole in the small capital, but she could economise on everything else, and he would get it laid before they moved in. The three went to their lunches, and she went into the garden and sat on a rickety garden seat and shared her sandwiches with Dusty, who was lolling happily in the unkept grass.

Mr Baxter had finished by mid-afternoon; Louise gave him a cheque and thanked him nicely. 'Do anything for a pretty young lady like you, miss,' mumbled Mr Baxter. 'Just you send along if you need any jobs done.'

'Oh, I will,' declared Louise, and beamed widely at him; life at Much Hadham was going to be a dream after Bick Street.

She made tea for Tim and Ted Poolley, and opened the packet of biscuits she had had the forethought to bring with her. The sitting-room was very nearly finished, and since Ted had promised the carpets would be laid within the week she would be able to stay at home and make the curtains. She saw them off home presently, tidied everything away, did what she could to tidy her own person and locked up. Ted had the second key, and she wouldn't be coming again until her last free day. She stood by the stout front door and surveyed her house with pride. Mr Baxter had seen to the windows, making them secure, and when they all came in a couple of days' time, they would clean windows. She sighed with con-

tent and turned round in time to see the doctor's Jaguar
slide to a halt by the gate.

Dr van der Linden got out, ushered Dusty on to the
back seat, stowed Louise's bits and pieces in the boot
and invited her to make herself comfortable beside him.

Louise, full of the false energy consequent on a sleep-
less night as well as a busy one, followed by a hard
day's work, was bright-eyed and chatty. He allowed
her to run on, merely murmuring placidly when she
paused for breath, and when they reached Bick Street,
despite the appearance of Zoë with an invitation to stay
for tea, he refused, although he qualified his refusal
with the suggestion that, once the family had settled in
their new home, Zoë might like to have tea with him.
'After all, I shall be a near neighbour,' he told her,
smiling down at the small, pretty creature.

Louise saw the smile; she wasn't at all surprised at
the effect Zoë was having on the doctor. She was
delightfully pretty, with a charming, unselfconscious
air. Louise, in the mental no man's land of one needing
her sleep, had the pair of them in love at second sight,
engaged and married even while she was bidding Dr
van der Linden a polite goodbye at her door; still in the
throes of romance, she watched Zoë accompany him
across the narrow pavement to his car. Provided he
wasn't married already, and she must discover that as
quickly as possible, he would do very nicely for her
sister—he was a lot older, of course, but that didn't
matter . . .

She dumped her boxes and bags in the kitchen,
greeted Mike and Christine, handed over Dusty to the
former for his walk, and sat down at the kitchen table.
Christine was sitting there, doing her homework, but

she paused to look at her elder sister.

'You're tired,' she declared. 'The kettle is boiling; I'll make tea—there is some cake . . . Then you go upstairs and lie down, Louise; Zoë and I will get the supper and call you when it's ready. We can talk then.'

Louise drank her tea and, urged by Christine, took herself off to her room. It overlooked the street and, glancing out of the window, she saw that the doctor was still talking to Zoë. Seeing them, she nodded with sleepy satisfaction and, kicking off her shoes, subsided on to the bed, to sleep within seconds.

Over supper, much refreshed, she described her day and discussed the weighty proble   of curtains. Since Zoë was free in the morning, they agreed to go together and buy all the material they needed. 'And on Saturday,' said Louise, 'we'll all go to Ivy Cottage and do the last odd jobs. I hope someone will buy those odds and ends of furniture before we move.' She ticked off everything which had to be done before they left Bick Street, and half-way through yawned prodigiously.

'You go to bed this instant,' said Zoë firmly. 'You're asleep on your feet. We'll make a list and you can check it in the morning.'

A good night's sleep worked wonders; Louise and Zoë, their list made to everyone's satisfaction, made their way to the High Street and spent an hour choosing material for the curtains. The windows of Ivy Cottage were small and the shop specialised in remnants; they returned home well pleased with themselves, laden with all they needed. It remained only to get the curtains made. In the cupboard under the stairs was a very old sewing machine; Louise hauled it out, set it to rights and, with Zoë to help her, got started.

They were all up early the next morning, and with Dusty and a number of bags, and a picnic lunch, they were at Ivy Cottage betimes.

Mr Poolley had been working hard. The lino on the kitchen floor was laid, the dining-room was carpeted and there was a sound of hammering from somewhere upstairs. With such an encouraging start to the day they set to work with a will and, by the time they left, the little house was beginning to look like home. Louise went on duty that evening feeling pleased and excited; in four days' time she would leave, and once they had settled into their new home she would go after a job.

Her euphoria waned a little as the night wore on. The medical wards were unusually busy; they were always full, but now they were spilling over, with extra beds up and a number of new patients who needed extra care. By the time she was due to go off duty she was tired and peevish, wanting her bed above all things.

It was nice to find breakfast ready and waiting when she got to Bick Street; her sisters and brother clustered round as she ate it, and only when she had finished did Zoë say, 'We knew you wouldn't mind, Louise—Dr van der Linden met me when I was out with Dusty yesterday evening—at least, he was driving home, I suppose, and came down this street . . . He stopped and asked if we wanted a lift tomorrow and I said yes.' She paused to look at Louise's face. 'You don't mind? It seemed such a splendid chance; we could start on the garden and he said we could have lunch at his house and take Dusty, so you'd have a nice long day to yourself. He'll bring us back this evening.'

Louise squashed a feeling of self-pity welling up in a threatening manner; it was kind of the doctor, and moreover it rather pointed to the fact that he had his eye on Zoë. Besides, if they went there for lunch they would soon know if he was married, in which case, the quicker he took his eyes off her, the better. In the meanwhile there was safety in numbers.

She said with an instant willingness that she didn't quite feel, 'What a splendid notion, my dears. Do remember to take Dusty's food with you and his bowl;' he'll be quite happy in the garden. Christine, if you finished your curtains yesterday evening, will you take them with you and hang them? There is a spade in the little garden shed at the end of the garden, but perhaps Dr van der Linden wouldn't mind you taking the garden fork—you could leave it there. Take a bottle of milk—you might want tea.' She saw their relief as she yawned and declared, 'Must say, a long sleep will be nice . . .'

'Then you don't mind—truly not?' asked Mike.

'Not one bit. I've had a rotten night—all go—and I can think of nothing nicer than a bath and bed. Take a key with you just in case I'm gone before you get back.' Something made her add, 'I told Night Sister on the surgical wards that I would cover for her for the first half-hour—she may be late on duty.'

Which wasn't true, but she had a reluctance to meet Dr van der Linden, although she wasn't quite sure why. Urged by the other three, she went upstairs to her room and got ready for bed but, although she was so tired, she was still awake when she heard the doctor's car stop and then the subdued, cheerful murmur of voices and Dusty's hastily suppressed barks. They would have a lovely day, she told herself with resolute cheerfulness. 'And I do hope he's not married,' she murmured as she dozed off.

CHAPTER THREE

IT WASN'T until the following morning when she reached Bick Street after another night of non-stop work that she had the details of the outing to Much Hadham, for she had prudently left some time before the working party would return. She hadn't seen Dr van der Linden, either, although he had been in the hospital to check on several very ill patients, but she had been busy at the time in the accident room and he had sent a message to say that he would leave instructions with the night nurse on duty and Ted Giles would get in touch with her as soon as she was free.

She found her brother and sisters in a high state of excitement; they had had a delightful day, they chorused, at the same time assuring her that they had worked like Trojans. Everything that needed to be done had been done, Zoë assured her, plying her with tea and toast, 'And we went to Aldo's house . . .'

'Aldo?'

Zoe laughed a little. 'That's his name, Dr van der Linden. He said it made him feel old when we called him doctor all the time. Well, it's at the other end of the village—his house—quite beautiful, Louise, and large with a huge garden at the back. It's old, eighteenth century, one of those with chequered brickwork, and inside it's furnished with the loveliest antiques. We only went downstairs, of course, but the hall is vast and there is a staircase, stone and wrought iron—there is a carpet on it, of course. We had a heavenly lunch . . .' She was interrupted here by Mike and Christine and a chorus of praise in which grilled mushrooms in a wine sauce, roast chicken and gooseberry tart with lashings of cream, and unlimited lemonade—the genuine kind, they explained—jostled in mouth-watering fashion.

Zoë went on just as though there hadn't been an interruption. 'And after lunch we went round the garden; it's beautiful, Louise, you have no idea . . .'

Louise said equably that no, she hadn't, and reflected silently that it seemed unlikely that she ever would, although . . . She allowed her thoughts to stray for a moment; if Dr van der Linden and Zoë should marry, she might be given the chance. And that reminded her.

'Did you meet his wife?' she asked with just the right amount of casualness.

'Wife? He hasn't got one. He has got a mother and father and brothers and sisters who live in Holland. His Granny was English; she left him that house. He has got degrees here and in Holland, but he works here, though he says he'll go back to Holland when he retires, or perhaps sooner.'

Dr van der Linden, who had never done more than pass the time of day with her, seemed to have been remarkably forthcoming about himself. Zoë would have charmed him into that, of course. Louise bestowed a motherly look on her young sister. No wonder he had been so obliging to herself, giving her lifts and sending the gardener's boy over to Ivy Cottage; he wanted an ally just in case Zoë might need an older sister's advice.

She took herself off to bed presently; Mike and

Christine had gone off to school, Zoë, reluctantly, to her secretarial college and, except for Dusty, the little house was empty. Forlorn, too, now, with books and china and all the odds and ends which had made it home packed away in boxes.

Two more days, thought Louise, lying half asleep in the bath, and they would be embarking on quite another way of life. She would miss her work at the hospital, of course, it had been satisfying, even if demanding, but she would find something just as interesting. A week, she mused, in which to get Ivy Cottage spick and span, and she would look for a job after that. Day duty, if possible. It was incredibly good luck that the Easter holidays were late this year; Christine and Mike had been accepted at schools at Bishop's Stortford, and would begin the summer term without too much of an upheaval, and Zoë, most fortunately, had taken her exams only that week and would, she hoped, be qualified to take a job. Life was spreading before her—all of them—in a splendid fashion. She supposed that it was because she was tired that she felt so low-spirited.

As though the hospital was reluctant to see her go, she was kept very busy for the next two nights, and although she saw Dr van der Linden on several occasions their conversation was kept strictly to his patients' treatment, and not one word did he let fall about anything else.

She left on her last morning, bearing various gifts from her nurses and the other night sisters and a multitude of good wishes, feeling as though she was living in a dream. A dream quickly dispelled once she got home, to find her brother and sisters in a high state of excitement. She finally got them away to her satisfaction to their various studies, and then took Dusty for a brisk walk around the uninteresting streets and returned home to start on the final packing.

There were still some curtains to finish; she decided to have an early lunch, go to bed for a couple of hours and get them done before the others came home. With Dusty for company she curled up on her bed and closed her eyes; she was on the point of sleep when the thought crossed her mind that Dr van der Linden hadn't wished her goodbye, nor for that matter had he expressed the hope that she would enjoy her future. They had never got beyond a cool friendliness, although she had known him for some years at the hospital; long enough for him at least to utter a token courtesy. Drifting off to sleep, she thought that she understood; of course, if he and Zoë were going to see a lot of each other, he would see her, too; there was no need to say goodbye.

She had the curtains ready by the time Mike and Christine got home; they took Dusty for his walk and Louise got the tea and presently Zoë got back, too, delighted that she had finished her course and brimming over with plans about a job. Cutting bread and butter while Louise warmed the teapot, she said happily, 'Aldo said I should get work quite easily; he said that Bishop's Stortford would be better than Stevenage, not as industrial; he said to try for a solicitor's office or a bank. He goes to Bishop's Stortford quite often; I can have a lift whenever I want one.'

'That's nice of him,' observed Louise in her calm way. 'I'm sure you'll find something quickly. Take a few days off first though, won't you?'

'Oh, rather, darling. We'll get Ivy Cottage just so before I start hunting for work. You must be tired. Can't you get a part-time job? I'll be earning too now, and there is no rent to pay, only rates. Is there any money left?'

'Not a great deal,' Louise's matter-of-fact voice sounded reassuring. 'Now we've got everything we need; I've put some money away to get Mike and Christine started—uniforms and so on—and I've a whole month's pay packet in my pocket. There is no need to rush off and take the first job that you are offered.'

Zoë said lightly, 'We could get married, that would solve that problem, only what would we do about Mike and Christine?'

Louise rammed the cosy down on the teapot. 'You get married, love, I'm quite happy as I am; I've been an old maid for so long now, I don't think I want to be anything else.'

Zoë chuckled. 'Idiot—you're twenty-six and quite beautiful.'

The move went without a hitch, largely due to Louise's sensible planning and the fact that Dr van der Linden telephoned minutes before the phone was cut off; Zoë answered his call and went dancing upstairs to where Louise was rolling up the last of the bed linen.

'That was Aldo. Isn't he a darling? He is going to Much Hadham in about half an hour, and says that he will take us and Dusty and drop us off at Ivy Cottage. That will leave you in peace to see the furniture out, won't it, Louise? The van driver will give you a lift, won't he?'

Louise knotted a stout cord around some blankets.

'Yes, dear. I am sure that he will. It would be a great help if Dr van der Linden would take you all, and Dusty, too. Have the men cleared downstairs yet? I told the landlord we would be out of here by eleven o'clock.'

'They were putting in the last few things when I came upstairs. Shall I start making the tea? They are bound to want a cup.'

'No, love, I'll do that just before we leave, but be a darling and put everything ready, will you? And mind you are all ready when Dr van der Linden gets here; he won't want to hang around.'

Zoë sped away and Louise, packing the very last odds and ends from the bedrooms, reflected that it was kind of Dr van der Linden to offer a lift. Of course, he was doing it so that he might see more of Zoë. She couldn't blame him; Zoë was so very pretty and sweet-natured.

The last chair was being stowed away when the landlord arrived for the key. Louise handed it over, listened kindly to his apologies and excuses, assured him that they had found somewhere else to live without saying where, and climbed into the van beside the driver and his mate. She didn't look back as they left Bick Street; it was a page in their lives she had turned with relief.

All the windows were open at Ivy Cottage, and as the van stopped Mike and Christine came running out. 'Zoë's just coming—we'll all help . . .'

The men wanted their lunch break; Louise invited them to sit where they liked to eat it, offered tea and then retired to the back garden where the four of them and Dusty ate the sandwiches she had prudently packed. It was delightful in the untidy tangle of greenery; they could have stayed there for the whole afternoon, but the sound of tramping feet sent them into the house to direct the men and help with the easier unloading. It was tea time when they finished and the van drove off, and Zoë, dropping into one of the shabby, comfortable armchairs in the sitting-room, exclaimed, 'I almost forgot. Aldo asked us all to go to his place for tea the minute the men went.' She jumped up again. 'I must wash and do my hair—Christine, Mike, tidy yourselves. Louise, you will love his house . . .'

'Some other time, dear.' Louise spoke with her usual serene voice. 'I'd much rather stay here; there are some papers I must get sorted before I lose track of them completely. Make my apologies, will you? I'll have a cup of tea soon. We will have supper about seven o'clock, shall we, and go to bed early? We've done enough for today.'

She watched them go presently, a little reluctantly because they didn't like leaving her behind, but they were accustomed to doing what she asked of them without demur; she was the head of the family, never unreasonable, seldom cross and always ready to help with their problems.

She put on the kettle, made some toast and sat down at the kitchen table to eat it, offering the crusts to the ever-hungry Dusty. She wondered briefly what the others would be having for tea and felt a small pang of envy—the envy, she reminded herself, was of the food, not of their host's company.

The doctor watched his guests coming along the street and a faint frown creased his handsome forehead, but his welcome was warm as they came in, and he didn't remark upon Louise's absence, but listened with casual good humour as Zoë explained why her sister had stayed behind, and made some equally casual remark about the cottage.

He gave them a gorgeous tea; scones and jam, thick cream, gingerbread, fruit cake, sandwiches and toast fingers spread with Gentleman's Relish.

Mike, a slice of cake half-way to his mouth, paused to say, 'This is the most super spread, sir; poor old Louise, missing it all.'

The doctor gave him a lazy smile. 'Well, we must try and make it up to her some time, mustn't we?' He turned to to Zoë. 'I don't know if you are interested but I had occasion to visit my solicitor today—he is looking for a typist. His office is in Bishop's Stortford; there's a staff of four or five girls, as well as a junior partner, and the pay is quite good. You would be the junior, of course.'

'Aldo, how marvellous—you really mean that?'

'I always mean what I say, Zoë. I'll let you have the address to write to; you will want to talk it over with Louise first, I imagine.'

'Oh, of course, but I know she will be over the moon —what a pity she isn't here now so that we could talk about it . . .'

'A great pity.' The doctor's voice was non-committal. 'But I'm sure she has more then enough to do at the moment.'

He made no move to detain them when they got up to go, but wished them a cordial good evening and went to the door with them, expressing the hope that he would see them again before very long, and he stood watching them going down the High Street, his thoughts miles away.

Louise received the news of a possible job for Zoë with her usual calm.

'It sounds just the thing, love. Do you know who to write to? It was kind of Dr van der Linden to think of you.'

'He said he's going to let me have the address; I do hope he won't forget.'

She need not have worried; the gardener's nephew came to the door the next morning with a brief note for Zoë; she sat down at once and wrote to the address which had been given to her and went down the street to the post office. She wondered if she should call at the doctor's house at the same time, but Louise had asked her to be quick because they had the rest of the unpacking to do. On her way back she fell to wondering if Louise liked Aldo; she had very little to say about him, and really there had been no reason why she shouldn't have gone with the rest of them to his house for tea.

Louise was arranging saucepans on a kitchen shelf, and Zoë, never one to hesitate, asked, 'Don't you like Aldo, Louise?'

Her sister was standing on a chair, the better to reach the shelf. She stood with a saucepan lid in her hand, and thought about it before answering matter-of-factly, 'I found him very nice to work for at the hospital and he has always been pleasant, but you see I don't know him as a person. I'm sure he is a very nice man—you like him, don't you?'

'Very much.' Zoë was putting mugs on a tray ready for coffee. 'I don't think "nice" describes him very well.' She glanced at her sister. 'He would make a marvellous husband.'

'I'm sure he would,' agreed Louise warmly; in her mind's eye she could see Zoë, a picture in white satin, walking down the aisle of St Andrew's church, with the doctor, the epitome of elegance, waiting for her; she must do all she could to turn the picture into reality.

She got off the chair. 'Let's have our coffee in the garden. I suppose Mike's in the attic with Dusty? And where is Christine?'

'Washing her hair. Is there enough money to get her uniform for school? And what about Mike?'

'There is enough, just. I thought I'd write around for a job while Christine and Mike are on holiday and before you get your job—I might be lucky enough to get an interview.'

She wrote that evening. Although Bishop's Stortford had nothing to offer her, Stevenage would like her to go along and have an informal meeting with the matron. A morning was suggested and Louise, very well dressed in her one good skirt and jacket, boarded the local bus. No mention had been made in the letter of a vacant post; perhaps they would merely make a note of her particulars and take her name in case something turned up.

Stevenage was a new town, given over largely to industry, and it had a great many factories. If she did get a job at the hospital, there would be plenty of work.

The interview went well; Louise, who had been expecting a youngish, very up-to-date matron, was surprised to find that lady elderly, not far off retirement, she guessed, and decidedly old-fashioned in her views. But the hospital was modern enough, well equipped, and the wards were bright and airy. Their tour took about half an hour, and at the end of it Louise was offered the post of day sister on women's medical.

'Shall we say a month's trial, Miss Payne? Before you sign a contract.' She added shrewdly, 'You may find me old-fashioned in my views; my nurses still wear caps and aprons, and since I am due for retirement in the next year or so, no one has objected; my successor will, no doubt, have her own ideas.'

She picked up Louise's references and read them for a second time. 'You are highly recommended,' she observed. 'Could you start as soon as the necessary paperwork has been done? That should take about a week.'

Louise went back home walking on air, her pretty head full of plans, plans she certainly wouldn't have been making if she had overheard the matron's long conversation on the telephone.

Zoë was out when she got home; shopping, said Christine. She and Mike received Louise's news with whoops of delight, and presently Louise told them to take Dusty for a walk. 'For I have to write and accept the job, and I'd better get it done at once.'

Not quite at once, though; the house had only been empty for five minutes and she was hunting for writing paper among the jumble of their possessions when the knocker was banged and, before she could answer it, Dr van der Linden walked in.

'Alone?' he asked blandly. 'If you haven't had coffee, I'd love some.'

Louise got up from her knees beside an unpacked tea chest. She said severely, 'Good morning, sir. Are you on holiday?'

'No, playing truant, merely.'

'In that case, I'll make the coffee.' She went through to the kitchen and found him at her heels. He looked around him with approval. 'You've made this little place very pleasant to live in,' he observed.

'Thank you. There is a good deal more to do still. I am sorry Zoë isn't here.'

She didn't see his surprised look and then the amusement gleaming in his eyes. 'Has she written about that job yet?'

'Oh, yes. I do hope she gets it. It was kind of you to tell her about it.'

'She is a very pretty girl.' He watched her from under heavy lids.

Louise's voice held warmth. 'Yes, isn't she? And such a nice person, if you know what I mean. I know she is only nineteen, but she is very mature—she'll make a splendid wife . . .'

'I couldn't agree more. Have you decided what you want to do, Louise?'

She handed him a mug of coffee and pushed the biscuit tin towards him. 'Well, I didn't need to decide. I wrote to Bishop's Stortford and Stevenage—they hadn't any vacancies at Bishop's Stortford, but I went for an interview at Stevenage this morning and I've been offered the day sister's post on women's medical —a month's trial before I sign a contract. I liked the matron and it's a busy hospital, isn't it?' She sugared her coffee. 'But of course, you wouldn't know that. I can't quite believe it, life has suddenly become almost too good to be true—everything I've wanted has dropped into my lap.'

'And what did you want?' He asked the question idly.

She waved an arm around the little kitchen. 'This—a home for us all—I mean, a real one that belongs to us, and decent schools for Mike and Christine, and fun for Zoë—there weren't many friends in Hoxton, and she's a friendly girl; I want her to have some pretty clothes and meet people and . . .'

She paused, and the doctor said quietly, 'Marry a man who will love her and make her happy.' And when she nodded, he added, 'And you, Louise, what do you want?'

'Me? But I have what I have always wanted. You asked me and I have just told you.'

'You have no wish to marry?'

She said in her sensible way, 'Well, who would look after the others, even if I knew a man who was prepared to take on four of us?' She added disarmingly, 'I don't know any men; night duty isn't conducive to social life.' She caught his eye and saw that he was amused, and said hastily, 'Oh, of course I know you and Dr Gillespie and Dr Foster and Dr Giles and the house doctors, but that is because I worked for you all.'

She took his mug and refilled it. 'What a funny conversation we're having. It was very kind of you to have the family over for tea—I haven't had a chance to thank you, but I do now.'

'My pleasure. You didn't come, Louise.' It was more a question than a statement.

'No—I had a lot to do.'

'That was the reason, was it? I thought that you might have been avoiding me.'

She went pink under his thoughtful eye. 'Why on earth should I do that?'

'I had no idea. I must go.' He glanced at his watch.

'I've a round this afternoon.' He added deliberately, 'Tell Zoë to let me know about that job. I am home most evenings after six or seven o'clock.'

He went away very quickly, leaving her feeling lonely, and at the same time pleased at his interest in Zoë.

The letter Zoë had hoped for came the next morning, and she caught the bus into Bishop's Stortford, leaving Louise to confer with the man from Telecom, who, when he heard that she was to work at the Stevenage hospital, professed his willingness to get a telephone laid on as quickly as possible.

No sooner had he gone than Miss Wills arrived on the doorstep. Louise made more coffee, for the Telecom man had finished the first lot, and sat down to listen to Miss Wills's gentle gossip. 'You managed your move very efficiently,' she observed approvingly, 'and how fortunate that dear Dr van der Linden was able to give you the opportunity of travelling with him. I chanced to meet him and mentioned that my sister had offered bed and breakfast to you all, and he assured me that he would be able to transport you all so that you wouldn't need to remain overnight here. Such a kind man.'

'Yes, he is,' agreed Louise. She told Miss Wills about her job in Stevenage and Zoë's hopes of working in Bishop's Stortford, and Miss Wills nodded approvingly. 'And while I'm here, may I ask if you have sold the furniture you didn't require? Our neighbour has built a small extension on to his house and needs a chair or two and a table.'

'They're still in the attic. I only sold the bed.'

'Then may I send him along? Your great-aunt always insisted on her furniture being well polished; I have no doubt that he will be very pleased to buy it.' Her gaze swept across the sitting-room. 'I see that you have kept several pieces . . . They are old-fashioned, of course.'

'Just right for this little house. You may be sure we'll take good care of them, Miss Wills. Do please send your neighbour along; he's most welcome to look at everything there is.'

Miss Wills took her leave. Louise watched her straight back disappear down the street and thought how delightful it was to be standing at her own front door. She patted the wall behind her lovingly and went back indoors to dust the furniture in the attic before Mr James arrived.

He came that afternoon, and she led him up the narrow stairs and showed him what there was; not a great deal—a few chairs, rather nice, well-made Victorian dining-chairs, none of them matching, a solid table with a chip out of one leg and some stains marring its oak surface, and a small cupboard, rather ornate. Mr James was determined to examine everything very slowly; a man slow to make up his mind, but at length he nodded. 'I'll take the lot for what you ask, but perhaps you will throw in that folding table in the corner there—it needs repairing but I'm a dab hand at that.' He made his rather ponderous way down to the hall. 'I'll come round with a hand cart and my son when he gets home this evening. You'll not need to lift a finger, young lady.'

Louise put the money he gave her into the china Toby jug on the kitchen dresser, where the housekeeping money was always kept. A new dress for Zoë, she decided happily, and Christine would be able to go on the school outing after Easter; the Head had sent a form when she had been accepted as a pupil and Louise had said that if she possibly could, Christine should go—now she would be able to. As for Mike, he had been hankering after a fishing-rod for months, even though there was nowhere to fish in Hoxton. He should have one now, and at the same time she would enquire where he could fish. There might be a few pounds over; she debated whether to get a bathmat for the bathroom or a blouse for herself. The bathmat won; she could get the blouse and even a dress with her first pay packet. Her suit was still good, and even though it was April and getting warmer by the day, she would be able to wear it for another month; it would be quite suitable to travel to and from the hospital in.

Mike and Christine came back then; she made coffee yet again and they went into the garden to drink it while Dusty lolled at their feet. She told them about the furniture and watched their faces light up. 'So you see, everything is simply splendid, my dears—Zoë will be back presently, and let's hope she has had the same sort of good luck.'

She was getting the lunch and the other two were in in the garden, starting on the weeding, when Zoë returned. The job was hers, she told them delightedly; she was to start on the following Monday and she would be paid weekly. There was a tennis club the other three girls in the office belonged to, and they had already asked her if she would like to join . . . She looked at Louise. 'But I said I'd let them know—there's an annual subscription and my tennis racquet needs some new strings.'

'You join, Zoë,' said Louise without hesitation. 'You'll make lots of friends and meet people. Have your racquet seen to and we'll kit you out.'

'But the money, Louise?'

'I've sold the bits and pieces in the attic; there is enough for you all to have something. Besides, we've both got jobs and there are still a few pounds left in the kitty.'

'Yes, but what about you?'

'I'll get some clothes when I get paid—I've plenty to go on with.'

'Well, mind you do,' said Zoë. 'Now, you must help me to dole out my salary. Where is some paper?'

The four of them sat around the table, discussing just how the money should be spent. They had it all nicely settled when Zoë said, 'I'll go and see Aldo this evening and tell hm about the job. He will be pleased.'

Which presently she did, not returning until Louise was on the point of dishing up their supper. 'He is awfully pleased,' she told them all. 'He persuaded me to stay and have a glass of sherry.'

'I bet you didn't need much persuading,' said Mike.

Zoë made a face at him. 'Silly, of course I didn't; he's lovely to talk to. This time I met his housekeeper, Mrs Potts—she is nice. Her husband works there too, a kind of butler, I suppose, although I didn't see him. Aldo says will we all go there for drinks on Saturday—six o'clock—he says there will be some people there who knew Great-Aunt Payne, and we might like to meet them. I said yes—was that OK?'

'Of course, love.' Louise was serving cottage pie and didn't look up. 'But count me out, I have to go to Stevenage to be fitted for my uniforms ready for Monday —not new ones, but they'll find something to fit and alter them. My appointment is for half-past five, so I can't get back in time. Make my excuses, my dears, and find out all you can about Ivy Cottage and Great-Aunt Payne.'

Her calm explanation satisfied everyone, although it wasn't strictly true; she did have an appointment at the hospital, but earlier in the afternoon, now she would have to telephone and alter it.

She rang up the next morning while the house was empty and got the time changed. Luckily there would be one worker left in the sewing-room until half-past five; she would have to be there at five o'clock sharp, she was told. Which meant that she would have to waste almost an hour before she caught the bus which would get her home too late to go to Dr van der Linden's house. She still had no clear idea why she had gone to so much trouble to avoid him, but she had too many other things to think about to worry over it.

Saturday came, and she took herself off to Stevenage. It was nice to have an hour or two to herself; she had spent days getting Ivy Cottage just so and, strong though she was, she was tired. She and Zoë had spent an afternoon in Bishop's Stortford so that Zoë could get a dress worthy of her job, and that morning the three of them had gone there again to buy the fishing-rod and some tights for Christine, leaving Louise to prepare a meal and take Dusty for a walk.

The talk over their meal was all of fishing and school outings and speculations as to Zoë's job which she was starting on Monday. It was fortunate that Louise's duty times were varied—she wouldn't need to go on duty until one o'clock on Monday and since Zoë would be home by six o'clock Christine and Mike would be alone for only a few hours. Shortly they would be going back to school and be away all day anyway. Louise, reviewing her carefully made plans, decided that they should work very well.

She was greeted sourly by the sewing woman at the hospital. 'Why you couldn't come earlier, I don't know,' she grumbled, 'and me with enough work on my hands for three; you should have been here at three o'clock . . .'

'Unforeseen circumstances,' observed Louise blithely, 'and we have half an hour before you go home. Is this the dress? I'll put it on at once, shall I?'

There wasn't much to be altered; indeed, they were finished with ten minutes to spare. Louise made short work of getting her own clothes on again, and the woman said grudgingly, 'I must say you've not fussed around—some of the nurses these days want this and that done . . . There will be a uniform and cap and aprons in your locker in the sisters' changing-room; you'll get the other two at the end of the week.'

Louise made her way to a café and sat drinking coffee for half an hour, and then, still with time on her hands, went through the shopping centre, planning the clothes she would buy once the family finances were on firm ground. The bus was full, but only a handful of people got off in the village; she exchanged goodnights with vaguely familiar faces and unlocked her front door, to be met by a delighted Dusty, bored with his own company.

There was a note on the kitchen table for her. 'Aldo says come over when you get back, before seven o'clock. Supper is in the Aga.'

It wasn't seven o'clock yet, but Louise had no intention of joining the party; to arrive late just as everyone was on the point of leaving wouldn't do at all. Besides, it was important that the doctor had no eyes for anyone but Zoë—not that he had eyes for herself, but common courtesy would necessitate him talking to her when he might have been talking to Zoë. Louise, her sensible head full of such foolish notions, went upstairs to take off her good suit.

The three younger ones came in on a wave of cheerful chatter and a good deal of laughter. They had had a marvellous time; Aldo had been super and the canapés had been out of this world. The other people there had been older but awfully kind, and they were sorry they hadn't been able to meet Louise. 'We excused you to Aldo,' said Christine, 'and he said to tell you that he hopes that you will be happy in your new job. He is going to St Nicholas's tomorrow for some meeting or other. Hard luck on a Sunday, isn't it?'

Louise, who had been conning various suitable speeches of regret to make if she should see him at church the next morning, said, 'Oh, very,' and heaved a sigh of relief. Later, getting ready for bed, she puzzled about that; she would have to meet the doctor again sooner or later, and surely it could be on their old cool and pleasant footing. 'I'm behaving like an absolute fool' she told herself, jumping into bed. 'He'll think I don't like him, and that won't do if he has fallen in love with Zoë.'

Several of the people who had been in the doctor's house at the party were in church, and after the service Zoë introduced her. There were younger men and women with them, too, all friendly, and when they parted Louise thought with satisfaction that here was a nucleus of young people for Zoë and Christine, and even a couple of boys Mike's age, as a start. And as for herself, the Vicar had invited himself to tea on her first afternoon off duty, and she had accepted an invitation to morning coffee on the following Saturday, when she wouldn't be on duty until one o'clock. Really life was perfect; well, almost, she amended, not knowing quite why.

Her working hours were already arranged, one o'clock until eight in the evening, or eight o'clock in the morning until three in the afternoon and two days off a week, and every other weekend these could be taken on Saturday and Sunday. After night duty, it would be as easy as falling off a log.

Cheered on her way by the encouraging goodbyes of the others, after an early lunch, she presented herself at the sisters' changing-room, donned her uniform, apron and little starched cap and went to Matron's office.

She wasn't there long; a few crisp words of welcome from that lady and she was taken to her ward, where she met the staff nurse who had been doing Sister's duties and the three nurses on duty with her.

Staff Nurse Miller was small and round and cheerful, and very relieved to hand over to Louise. 'I'm to stay on until five o'clock, Sister,' she explained, 'so you can see the reports and meet the patients— there are twenty-four of them—we are nearly always full. Would you like to do a round first? It's tea for the sisters at four o'clock,' she observed, 'when you came back there will just be time for us to do another round if you like, Sister.'

'Where do I go for tea?' asked Louise.

'Oh, to the ground floor, take the left-hand passage, it's the door at the end.' She added encouragingly, 'They are all nice, the sisters.'

Which proved true enough. Louise was made welcome and sped back to the ward feeling that she was going to enjoy working with such a friendly crowd. There were several ill patients, ill enough to merit the visits of the house physician and then the medical registrar, and when old Mrs Trott collapsed an hour after Staff Nurse Miller had gone off duty Louise summoned medical help once more; unless she was mistaken, the old lady had had a cerebral haemorrhage.

The registrar, a fussy, pompous little man whom Louise was very afraid she wasn't going to like, agreed with her. 'I have been afraid of this,' he told her. 'Mrs Trott has had two similar episodes.' He fingered his lip and looked wise. 'I shall inform the consultant physician and take his advice.'

Passing the buck, thought Louise, going about the task of keeping Mrs Trott alive; she was familiar with the routine and she saw no reason why her patient should not recover for a third time; she wasn't in a deep coma and her pulse was strong. She was making out the necessary charts beside the bed while the nurses tidied the ward for the night, when there was a murmur of voices and a moment later the cubicle curtains were swept aside and Dr van der Linden, with Dr Cooper at his heels, came quietly to the bedside.

CHAPTER FOUR

DR VAN DER LINDEN nodded briefly at Louise, who only stared back at him, holding back the riot of mixed feelings at his arrival. His 'Good evening, Sister Payne, I'll just take a look, if I may?' was uttered in his usually pleasant cool manner.

Dr Cooper began, 'Sister Payne has taken over Sister Tomkin's post; she . . .'

Dr van der Linden interrupted briskly. 'Sister and I are already acquainted. Now, if I may have the notes?'

Mrs Trott was very ill, but by no means past aid; presently Dr van der Linden straightened his back, ramming his stethoscope into a jacket pocket. 'Has intensive care been warned?'

'Yes, sir.' How easy it was to slip back into their old professional relationship.

'Good. Let's have her up there, shall we?' He turned his head and watched the night nurses coming on to the ward. 'Sister, I expect you will want to give the report, but I would be glad if you will supervise Mrs Trott's removal first. I'll go ahead and have a word . . .'

He left then, taking the pompous Dr Cooper with him. Louise sent the nurses off duty, asked the senior night nurse to wait for the report, and then borrowed the junior to help her. The porters came then, and the next ten minutes or so were taken up with Mrs Trott being settled and connected up to the various devices which, hopefully, would revive her. Another ten minutes were taken up in conferring with the staff nurse on duty in the intensive care ward before Louise felt free to return to her own ward and give the report. By the time she had done that it was almost nine o'clock; if she hurried she would be able to get the last bus home. She tidied the books on her desk and got up just as the door opened and Dr van der Linden came in.

He said without preamble, 'I'll take you back. I telephoned Zoë and told her that you would be late. I'll be outside in ten minutes.'

He was gone without giving her a chance to answer. Over and above her annoyance at his arbitrary manner was relief that she wouldn't have to race like a mad woman for the last bus. She wished the night nurse goodnight and, bearing in mind the doctor's words, hurried down to the changing-room.

Dr van der Linden was standing in the forecourt talking to Dr Cooper, but as she went through the door he nodded to his registrar and opened his car door for her.

She settled in the comfortable seat with an unconscious sigh; she was tired and hungry, and only too thankful to sit still for a short while.

'Thrown in at the deep end, weren't you?' remarked her companion.

'Yes. I had no idea that you had beds here.'

'Why should you have? I don't remember telling you that I had.'

She said stiffly, 'I'm sorry, I had no intention of being nosy.'

He ignored that. 'Are you hungry? Did you get your supper?'

'No—I don't have it at the hospital. Normally I would be able to get the twenty-past-eight bus.' She added politely, 'This is very kind of you, Dr van der Linden.'

They were already at Much Hadham. 'I told Zoë you would be having supper with me.'

Without asking her first! Louise said tartly, 'Most kind of you, but if you don't mind, I prefer to go straight home. Some other time . . .'

He said silkily, 'Oh, but I do mind, and some other time covers so many things, does it not? The hair must be washed, the kitchen floor must be scrubbed, the dog must be taken for a run. I do not know why you are avoiding me, Louise, but if you have developed a sudden dislike of me after all this time, do say so; I find this maidenly shrinking from my company tedious. But if you can bear with me, Mrs Potts will give us supper and you can be home and in bed by eleven o'clock at the latest.' He stopped before his front door. 'Zoë told me to tell you that she would see that the young ones went to bed on time, and that it would be a good thing if you had supper with me because she had burnt the casserole she had saved for you.'

Louise chuckled. 'Put like that, how can I refuse?' She added a little shyly, 'I don't dislike you, Dr van der Linden.'

He undid her seat belt, got out and opened her door. 'Good, and since we are to be friends, could you not call me Aldo like the rest of your family?'

His door had been opened by a short, stout man, and he said, 'Ah, Potts, I've brought Miss Payne back for supper. Louise, this is Potts, who runs my home with his wife, and remarkably well they do it, too.'

Potts smiled in an indulgent way, and wished Louise a good evening. 'And ask Mrs Potts if she will come and take care of Miss Payne, will you? Supper in ten minutes or so?'

'Ten minutes, Mr Aldo; I've put the drinks in the drawing-room.'

Potts trod silently away to the back of the wide hall and through the baize door beside the staircase, curving up the wall to the gallery above. Louise looked around her. Zoë had been quite right; if the hall was anything to go by, the house was a delight. The floor was polished wood, the walls papered in golden yellow, echoing the pale colours of the Savonnerie carpet. There was a fireplace between the doors on one side of the hall, with a steel grate and an old-fashioned fender, and above it a large oil painting of a rural view. Facing the fireplace was a small wall table bearing a bowl of spring flowers and flanked by two leather-covered Regency chairs; there were doors on this side, too, heavy mahogany with brass handles. Aldo opened the nearest now and a St Bernard dog bounced through to rear up on his hind legs to greet his master.

'Bernie,' said Aldo, 'come and say hello to Louise.'

The great dog transferred his attentions to her and she cried, 'Oh, you gorgeous beast,' and hugged him, almost staggering against his weight, but at a quiet word from the doctor he sat back, his tongue lolling as Mrs Potts came into the room.

'Ah, Mrs Potts, see that Miss Payne has all she needs, will you?' He glanced at Louise. 'I'll be in the drawing-room.' He nodded towards a door on the other side of the hall.

In the well-appointed cloakroom tucked away under the stairs, Louise did what she could to improve her appearance. She surveyed her somewhat washed-out reflection with distaste, powdered her nose, used lipstick and combed her hair, and then went back into the hall. The doctor opened a door wide as she did so and ushered her into his drawing-room.

She stood just inside the door and gazed round her. 'Oh, what a beautiful room,' she said softly, and indeed it was. Raspberry-coloured walls, bare save for several gilt-framed paintings, a sage-green carpet with the texture of velvet, easy chairs covered in chintz—a cream background patterned with pink and red roses and green foliage—and two large couches upholstered in a velvet which matched the walls exactly. The curtains of the same chintz, the swags above them lined with red satin, tied back with matching cords and tassels. There was a large rococo mirror over the plain marble fireplace, and cream shaded lamps on the small tables scattered around.

'Come and have a drink,' suggested Dr van der Linden, and she sat down with a small sigh of pleasure.

She said in her sensible way, 'Of course, you are used to it, but to anyone coming in here for the first time, it's—it's like a lovely dream.'

'I am glad you like it.' He handed her a drink and sat down in one of the armchairs with Bernie beside him, watching her face. When she opened her mouth to speak and then closed it again firmly, he smiled faintly. 'My mother is English and I was born in Holland, but my grandmother left me this house when she died, and as I spent a good deal of time here when I was a child and later when I came over here to take an English degree, I already had a great love of it, so I have made it my home.'

The sherry was warming Louise's insides nicely. 'But don't you miss your home in Holland?'

He shrugged. 'I am able to go there very frequently —indeed, I occasionally go there to lecture and examine—and my parents visit me often.' He got up and took her glass. 'Shall we have supper?'

The dining-room was across the hall. Here the walls were amber silk, and over the chimneypiece there was a lighted painting of a family group. The curtains were of the same colour as the walls, and the floor was carpeted in a rich brown. There were candelabra on the mahogany table and on either side of the chimneypiece, and a small bowl of spring flowers on the table, which was laid with Spode china. There were linen place mats flanked by plain silver and shining glassware. Louise sat down opposite her host and ate her supper with a sharpened appetite, a little surprised to find that they had a good deal in common and that talking to him became easier by the minute while they enjoyed French onion soup, ate sole *bonne femme* with a variety of delicious accompanying vegetables, and finished with a lime soufflé.

Mindful of her hopes for Zoe's future, Louise talked about her as much as possible, and was pleased to see that the doctor shared her interest. He agreed with her that Zoë was a very pretty girl and volunteered the information that she would make a good wife; he said so seriously, but there was a gleam of amusement in his eyes which she didn't see. With a startled eye on the clock, Louise drank her coffee and said that she must go home.

'I'm on at eight o'clock,' she remembered. 'I'm not used to day duty times yet.' She offered a hand. 'Thank you for a delicious supper and for bringing me home.'

He went to the door with her, and then through it and on to the pavement. 'A breath of fresh air is pleasant in the late evening,' he told her blandly, and walked her through the village to her own door, carrying on a placid conversation about nothing much. At the gate Louise said, 'I'm afraid Zoë will be in bed . . .'

He said easily, 'Her first day at work she will be tired, I dare say. Will you tell her that I have to go to Saffron Walden early tomorrow? If she can get to my place by eight o'clock, I'll give her a lift. I can't hang around, though, for I have to be at St Nicholas's by ten o'clock.'

'I'll tell her.' She put out her hand. 'You have been very kind to us, Doctor—Aldo, and I do thank you.' She opened the door. 'Goodnight.'

Zoë wasn't in bed. She was in her dressing-gown, curled up in the comfy old chair by the Aga, with Dusty curled up beside her. She yawned and smiled. 'I couldn't go to bed until I'd seen you, Louise. I wanted to tell you about my day and hear about yours. Did you have a good supper with Aldo? Isn't his house super? I've had a lovely day; they are all so nice at the office and I managed quite well, I think. The girls are dears and there is a junior partner . . . I did some letters for him. His name is George Standish, he lives in Bishop Stortford, he asked me if I was going to join the tennis-club.' She grinned happily. 'He's very good-looking.'

She got up. 'I'll make a cup of tea. 'Have you had a busy day? Aldo said on the telephone that there had been a hitch.'

Louise wondered if Mrs Trott would mind being called a hitch. She said in her quiet way, 'Yes, there was a hitch, but otherwise the day went very well. I think I shall like working there.'

'Did you have a lovely supper?'

'Yes, I did. Dr van der Linden has a beautiful house—what I saw of it. Now, tell me some more about your job, it sounds great.'

Zoë rattled on and Louise sipped her tea and thought about Dr van der Linden; he had been very forthcoming about his private life during the evening— possibly, she reflected, to give her some idea of his life-style and allow her to see what it was and that Zoë would be cared for in a more than adequate manner; she was, after all, *in loco parentis*. He would be a good husband; she would have preferred someone younger for Zoë, but one couldn't have everything . . .

'What are you thinking about?' asked Zoë with a touch of impatience. 'I've been telling you about Mr Standish and I don't believe you have heard a word.'

'Oh, yes, I did,' declared Louise mendaciously. 'He does sound great.'

They went to bed presently, and in the morning Louise left the other three still sleeping and caught her early-morning bus to Stevenage.

Her day was a busy one, full of small setbacks; a nurse off sick, Mrs Trott still very poorly in intensive care, several ladies under the impression that a new sister on the ward might give them an opportunity to complain about their medicines, their diets and the way the night nurses would wake them too early in the morning, all of whom had to be listened to, soothed

and assured that everything they were ordered was
exactly right for them, and over and above these tiresome things there were visits from the house
physician and another from Dr Cooper, who prosed
on and on at each bedside, using long words the
patients didn't understand, so that when he went at
last Louise had to do a round, reassuring them that his
oratorical display was merely their various illnesses
translated into medical terms.

There had been a vague hope that Dr van der Linden
might pay a visit, but from casual tactful questioning
of the house physician she discovered that he did a
weekly round and came when requested to do so. 'Dr
Cooper sent for him yesterday because last time Mrs
Trott collapsed he wasn't quite satisfied . . .'

He didn't say why, and Louise did not ask.

Staff Nurse Miller took over at three o'clock, and
Louise, with half an hour before her bus went, did
some shopping for supper. On the bus presently she
thought with satisfaction that the duty hours suited
her very well; it would take her a little while to get into
the swing of things, but already she was planning the
days. She was free now until one o'clock the next day,
which would give her ample time to catch up with the
household chores. Christine was splendid at doing the
ironing and getting her and Mike's midday lunch, but
they were both busy setting their rooms to rights,
besides doing the local shopping and taking Dusty for
his walks. Once they were at school it would, in a
way, be easier. Dusty would have to be left alone
during the mornings when she was on duty early and
for an hour or two on alternate afternoons, but then
Christine and Mike would be home before five

o'clock. She got off the bus, opened her door and went inside.

At a glance, the note on the kitchen table informed her that Christine and Mike had taken Dusty for a walk and would be back in time for tea, with a strong hint that they would be hungry by then. Louise changed into a dress she kept to wear in the house, and set about cutting bread and butter and making sandwiches. There was no cake left; she made a batch of scones, and while they baked she carried the tea-tray through to the dining-room and laid the table. Great-Aunt Payne had left some pretty china in the sideboard there; Louise got out the cups and saucers of blue and white Bow china, some of them cracked and chipped, but none the less charming, and went to butter the scones. She had just finished when Dusty and Christine and Mike returned.

They sat over their tea; there was such a lot to talk about—the new schools, Louise's job, Zoë's good luck in finding work so quickly, the things which still had to be done in the house. They were still there when Zoë came home. She didn't come into the house at once, but stood at the door talking, and Louise heard the doctor's deep voice answering and then Zoë's laugh. She looked anxiously at the almost empty plates; if he stayed for tea—although it was now a bit late—he would have to make do with the packet of rich tea biscuits she kept for emergencies . . .

Zoë shut the door and Louise heard the car drive away as Zoë came dancing into the room. 'I've had tea,' she said at once. 'Aldo picked me up from the office and we stopped at a funny little place just outside Bishop's Stortford and had a great big pot of tea and the loveliest Madeira cake . . . He wouldn't come in—he thought you might be tired, Louise.'

'How very considerate of him,' observed Louise in an equable voice which betrayed nothing of her feelings; the remark made her sound as though she was only just holding her own under the burden of a job, a house to run and a family to care for. An exaggeration which she was able to laugh about in the light of morning.

During the next week or so she saw Dr van der Linden only once, and that was when he did his weekly round of her ward. His manner had been exactly right; politely casual between the beds and strictly professional at the patients' bedsides. Even though he had had the opportunity to speak to her in private if he had been so minded, he hadn't, merely wishing her good day and walking away with Dr Cooper, his house physician and all the rest of them trailing behind him.

He was deliberately avoiding her, Louise decided, for the rest of her family mentioned him frequently enough; he had given Zoë several lifts to and from work; Mike and Christine had seen him on various occasions driving through the village, and each time he had stopped to speak to them. She racked her brain, trying to think what she might have said or done to annoy him, but she could think of nothing.

She arrived home after a particularly busy day to find the house empty and a laconic note, 'Gone fishing', on the kitchen table. There was a letter addressed to herself beside it, and she opened it idly. It was an invitation to attend the Spring Ball which was held at St Nicholas's Hospital in ten days' time, and enclosed with it was a note from Matron, hoping that she would attend and renew her various friend-ships.

It would be fun to go, thought Louise, but she didn't think she would go, all the same. True, she had last year's dress hanging in the wardrobe, rather out of date but still passable, and it would be nice to see her friends again, but supposing no one asked her to dance, and how was she to get back to Much Hadham afterwards? She put the card back in its envelope and made a pot of tea.

'There was a letter for you,' said Christine as they all sat round the table at supper that evening.

'Only an invitation to the St Nicholas Spring Ball,' said Louise, dishing out shepherd's pie.

There was a concerted chorus of, 'You must go; when is it?'

'Ten days' time, but I'm not going.'

'You can have a new dress; I'll let you have my week's wages,' offered Zoë.

Louise thanked her warmly. 'Thank you, darling. But I'm not going.' Nothing any of them could say changed her mind. Tomorrow morning she would write and decline, and post the letter before she went to the hospital at one o'clock.

She wrote it directly after breakfast the next morn-ing, after Zoë had gone and Christine and Mike had taken Dusty for his morning walk. It was a pleasant day, and a walk to the post office would be nice—she fetched a jacket and started off briskly. She had gone only a hundred yards or so down the main street when she saw Dr van der Linden bearing down towards her, quite obviously intent on speaking to her. He fetched up in front of her, blocking her path so that she had to stop.

'Good morning, Louise. I was on my way to see you.' His eyes rested on the envelope in her hand and he took it quite gently from her and read the address. 'Have you accepted?' he wanted to know.

She put out a hand to take it back and thought better of it.

'Very wise,' he said softly. 'It would hardly do to have a tussle in the centre of the village. You haven't answered my question.'

'I've refused.'

'How very fortunate that I should reach you before you arrived at the post office. It would give me great pleasure if you would come with me, Louise.'

She stared up at him. 'To the ball? To St Nicholas's? As your partner?'

'Why so surprised? It seems to me to be a most convenient arrangement; we can go and return together, thus solving the question of travel for you, and giving me the pleasure of a charming partner for the evening. Although I shan't take umbrage if you should choose to dance with anyone else.'

'Well,' said Louise, 'well . . .' She stood thinking about it. 'You're sure it's me you want to take? Why?'

'Did I not make myself clear? You are known to everyone at the hospital; so am I. What could be more natural than us going together? After all, we live within sight of each other's front doors.' He smiled suddenly. 'Besides, I should hate to go without a partner . . .'

'But you would have plenty—all the doctors' wives and Matron and the sisters . . .'

'If you are with me, I'll only need to do my duty dances once.'

'Oh, so that is what we were.' She spoke tartly.

'Not all of you.' He smiled slowly and she went faintly pink. 'Please come, Louise?'

She hesitated. 'Zoë . . .' she began.

'No, she knows no one at St Nicholas's, does she? It wouldn't be much fun for her—you have friends enough who will be delighted to see you again.'

'Well, it would be nice . . . Very well, I'll come.'

He didn't let her have her letter back. 'Splendid. Come back home and write an acceptance. I'll let you know at what time I'll pick you up—we're bound to see each other from time to time; if not, I'll telephone.'

He turned her round smartly and started walking back towards Ivy Cottage. 'You're free until midday? Good. Zoë was telling me that you've uncovered some rather nice rose bushes in the garden; if you invite me for coffee I'll take a look at them and tell you what they are.'

'Do you know?'

'I'll let you know that when I've seen them.'

She had intended to turn out the linen cupboard, still rather chaotic after the move, and there was a load of washing to hang out before she left the house. The linen could wait, she had a day off the next day, and Christine would hang out the washing. She led the way indoors, through the cottage and out into the garden. The roses, hitherto hidden in coarse clumps of grass and massive weeds, were more or less standing free once more, and all of them had foliage.

'I'll put on the kettle,' said Louise, and left him there while she got mugs and milk and sugar and inspected the tin of biscuits.

He wandered in presently. 'Quite a nice selection,' he observed, and went to wash his earthy hands at the sink. 'An Iceberg, two Super Star, a Queen Elizabeth and a Wendy Cussons. They are in good heart; it's too late to prune them though, and they will need some surface mulch; may I send the boy over with some? We have more than we need. He could help Mike dig it in.'

'That's kind of you, but I'll send Mike over for it, shall I? I'm sure . . .'

Mike and Dusty, followed at a more leisurely pace by Christine, came into the kitchen at that moment. They greeted the doctor like an old friend, and took him outside again to examine the garden and boast of the work they had done there. And since they showed no signs of coming in again Louise took the tray of coffee outside and set it on the rickety table by the shed. The doctor didn't stay long, and since the talk was taken up entirely by gardening nothing more was said about the ball.

As soon as he had gone, Louise sat down and wrote her acceptance, while Christine hung over her shoulder, advising her what to wear, how to arrange her hair and the right shade of lipstick. 'You're really very pretty,' she declared, 'and it doesn't show at all that you're twenty-six.'

A remark which Louise took in good part, with a meek promise to buy another lipstick.

During the next few days she toyed with the idea of buying a new dress for the ball, but if she did it would make a hole in her bank account, and really last year's was not too bad. Besides, she doubted if Dr van der

Linden would notice what she was wearing, and he certainly wouldn't remember that he had seen the dress already at last year's ball.

She had arranged her days off to coincide with the date of the ball so that she was able to spend a few leisurely hours washing her hair, doing her nails and examining her pretty face for wrinkles and spots. She had seen very little of the doctor, but he had phoned to say at what time he would call for her, and Zoë, who saw more of him than anyone else, declared that he was looking forward to the evening. 'It's so handy,' she explained as she helped with the washing up. 'Aldo goes to Bishop's Stortford quite often, you know, and it's great getting a lift.' She polished a plate with unnecessary care. 'Louise, do you mind if Mr Standish comes for me on Saturday? He thinks it would be a lot easier for me if he took me to the tennis club and I met everyone . . .'

'A splendid idea, love. You will make heaps of friends. Does Aldo belong to the club, too?'

'No, worse luck, he says he hasn't the time, though Mr Standish told me that he is an awfully good player. He plays squash, too.' She added, 'Of course, when you are getting towards middle age you need to keep fit.'

Louise wrung out the dishcloth. 'He's not quite as old as that, surely?' She frowned at the thought. 'Does he seem old to you, Zoë?'

'Good heavens, no. He's great fun—I adore him.'

A satisfactory answer which should have afforded Louise a good deal of pleasure, and which, unaccountably, did not . . .

The dress, amber crêpe, well cut and an excellent fit,

looked all right when she got into it, although she was only too well aware that in the ballroom it would go unremarked among the high fashion worn by the ladies present. She spent an anxious few minutes looking for the angora stole which would do duty as an evening wrap, presented herself for inspection under Christine's critical eyes and Zoë's comforting praise, and went into the sitting-room where the doctor was waiting. He looked up from the book on fishing Mike was showing him, wished her a grave good evening and then smiled.

'You look charming,' he told her.

'Oh, good,' said Louise cheerfully. 'It's last year's, you know. You wouldn't have noticed that I wore it at the last ball.'

He did not contradict her, but his eyes gleamed with amusement. He looked remarkably handsome himself, thought Louise, wrapping herself into the stole; a dinner-jacket suited him and, though she didn't know much about such things, it seemed to her that his was superbly tailored. He would have to have everything made for him, of course, she reflected, an admiring eye on his snowy shirt-front, for he was such a very large man.

The drive to the hospital was accomplished in a pleasant atmosphere of casual friendship; beyond one or two remarks, the doctor showed no interest in Louise's work although he seemed willing enough to discuss Zoë's job. 'She seems to be doing very well,' he observed. 'It is a pity that bright young things like her all too soon get married.'

'I don't think that is a pity,' declared Louise. 'You said yourself that she would make a good wife.'

'Indeed, yes. One man's loss is another man's gain. She has a most endearing personality.'

'Yes, hasn't she?' Louise sounded as though she meant it, and she did. 'It's such a pity she couldn't have come to the ball in my place.'

'You have no wish to come?' The doctor's voice was silky.

'Of course I have. It will be lovely to see everyone again. Only I don't want her to miss any fun . . .'

'And have you not missed a good deal of fun yourself during the last few years, Louise?'

She said stiffly, 'That's got nothing to do with it.'

He didn't answer, only remarked presently on the fine evening and the prospect of good weather. Always a safe topic, thought Louise, answering in kind.

The ball was held in the lecture hall of the hospital, suitably decked for the occasion with balloons, a good deal of crêpe paper and a great many artificial flowers. It was well under way by the time they arrived, and Louise, going to the side room set apart for the ladies' wraps, could hear the band pounding away at the other end of the hall. The doctor was waiting for her when she emerged; she looked elegant and with not a hair out of place, and definitely worth a second glance, even if her dress wasn't in the forefront of fashion.

She said in her matter-of-fact way, 'Am I all right?' and since she was peering over his shoulder at the half-open door and the mass of dancers beyond, she missed his look, although she heard his bland, 'Perfectly all right, Louise.'

They shook hands with the dignitaries, and Louise spent a few minutes with Matron, while Dr van der

Linden exchanged brief greetings with those of his colleagues who were in the reception committee, before scooping her up and dancing her off to join the crowd on the floor.

They danced together for half an hour or more, until Ted Giles tapped the doctor on the shoulder. 'May I have just one dance with Louise, sir?' he asked, and she found herself dancing off with Ted, and a moment later saw Dr van der Linden partnering the medical consultant's wife. Of course he would have to dance with his colleagues' wives—Matron, too, and the wives and daughters of the hospital committee. She doubted if she would see much more of him that evening.

Which proved to be the case, although he took her in to the supper room and sat for half an hour with her eating minuscule sausage rolls, very small sandwiches and ice-cream, making the kind of small talk generally found at social occasions. It was a relief to her when the medical registrar came across and reminded her that she had promised him a dance. A few minutes later she saw the doctor with Matron, and it wasn't until the last dance was announced that he appeared beside her, and without speaking waltzed her off. As they circled the ballroom, she reflected that it had been a pleasant enough evening; it had been fun to meet her friends again, and her dress had gone unremarked in the crush. She would have liked to have danced more often with the doctor; he was a good dancer and so was she; a sufficient reason for the regret she felt.

There was some delay before they left: friends to seek out and bid goodbye, Matron to thank, several of the medical staff to exchange polite nothings with, but they left at last, got into the car and began the drive back to Much Hadham.

It was a clear night, with the moon sailing through a starry sky, and there was little traffic; they talked in a desultory fashion about the evening, and when Louise stifled a yawn the doctor said, 'Off duty tomorrow, Louise?'

'Yes, and a good thing, too. Are you? Free, I mean?'

'No, I'm going to Leeds Infirmary to give a couple of lectures.'

'You're not driving there?'

'Why ever not?' His voice was cool. 'I don't have to lecture until the early afternoon.'

'But it's past two o'clock. You'll never get there . . .'

'I will leave around eight o'clock and be there for lunch.'

She persisted, 'But it's over a hundred and seventy miles, isn't it?'

'About that, I think. I appreciate your concern, Louise, but you have no need to fuss.'

A remark which caused her to retreat into peevish silence, a silence only broken when he stopped in front of Ivy Cottage.

'Would you like to come in for a cup of coffee?' she asked.

'It's rather late—or should I say early? Some other time, if I may?'

He had got out and taken her key to open the door.

'It was a lovely evening, thank you very much,' said Louise, sounding like a polite little girl leaving a party.

'Indeed a lovely evening, Louise, and it is I who thank you for it.'

He took her hand briefly, and then opened the door

so that there was nothing for it but to go past him into the hall. She stood behind the closed door, listening to the car being driven away. She hadn't thought much about it, but she hadn't expected the evening to end like that, almost as though he was glad it was over. Perhaps he was. She crept up to bed, vaguely troubled.

The ball was discussed *ad nauseum* the next day, and the following day she went on duty at eight o'clock, glad that she had a day's work to occupy her mind.

She had done her morning round, assigned the day's work to her nurses, and was in her office catching up on the paperwork when the phone rang. Matron would like to see her in the office.

Louise handed over to Staff Nurse Miller and started off through the hospital corridors. It would be about signing her contract; her month would be up in a few days' time, and once she had signed she would have to give three months' notice if she wished to leave. The job wasn't precisely what she would have chosen; her work had been much more varied at St Nicholas's and more interesting. On the other hand, she had security and no money worries; very likely she would continue in the same job for years. The thought depressed her just a little; one should be thankful for the way things had turned out. She knocked on Matron's office door.

Matron looked uneasy, but she invited Louise to sit down, enquired as to whether she had enjoyed the ball, remarked in passing that Louise was running her ward well and then, after a lengthy pause, said, 'The hospital governors had a meeting this week; there will have to be certain retrenchments made, Sister Payne.

Cutting down on staff is to be one of them. I am sorry to tell you that you are to be made redundant.'

Louise felt the shock of the words running through her like ice-cold water. She heard herself speak in a quiet voice. 'I'm sorry to hear that, Matron, but I quite understand—I have no contact and obviously I should be one of the first to go.'

'How sensible of you to see that at once, Sister.' Matron sounded very relieved. 'Needless to say, I am very sorry to lose you. I am more than satisfied with your work, but I have no say in the matter. Your ward is to be combined with the men's medical under one sister—Sister Crewe has been here for many years, of course.'

She waited for Louise to speak and, when she didn't, 'You have less than a week, have you not? Please come and see me again before you leave, and of course I shall be only too pleased to give you a reference. You must let me know if I can help in any way.'

Louise thanked her and went back to the ward. She got through the day somehow, and went home thankful that it was Christine and Mike's first day at their new schools. She had the house to herself, with Dusty for company. She sat for a long time on the stairs, crying all over his coat.

CHAPTER FIVE

IT WAS Dusty who brought Louise's fit of weeping to an end. He was devoted to Louise, but he disliked the dampness engendered by her tears. He wriggled free and she said apologetically, 'Sorry, Dusty—so silly of me,' and got up and washed her face and set about getting tea ready. By the time the others got in she was her usual serene self, although her eyelids were red and so was the tip of her pretty nose.

It was Christine who asked at once, 'What's the matter, Louise?'

Louise handed round the cups of tea. 'My dears, bad news, I'm afraid—they're cutting down at the hospital and I'm out of a job in a few days' time.'

'But they can't . . .' There was a chorus of indignation.

'Oh, yes, they can. I'm the last to be offered a job at the hospital, so it's only fair that I should be the first to depart.' She looked at their anxious faces. 'Don't worry, my dears, I'll get another job—there's no need to worry. We have a home of our own and Zoë has a job, and you two are at school and there is still some money in the bank.'

She watched them relax, and then Zoë asked, 'Shall I give up the tennis club—I could, you know; I haven't paid my sub yet . . .'

'I don't need to go on that outing,' declared

Christine stoutly.

'Thank you both, but there is no need to change anything; there's enough tucked away to keep us comfortably for several months.' A gross exaggeration if ever there was one; indeed a fib, but there would be a job of some sort, there was bound to be.

She handed over her ward without fuss, bade the other sisters goodbye, assured Matron that she would find another post without difficulty, and left the hospital as quietly as she had entered it only a brief month previously.

She had seen Dr van der Linden once more on the ward when he did his weekly round, but she had said nothing to him; moreover she had told Zoë that on no account was she to mention the matter to him. He had greeted her in his usual calm way, dealt with his patients, given her instructions and gone on his way. She had watched him go, suppressing a strong wish to run after him and tell him all about it. Doubtless in due course he would be told, but with any luck, by the time she saw him again, she would have found another post, or at least applied for one.

It seemed rather strange to be at home all day, but rather nice, too. She finished the last of the cupboards, got on with the garden, took a delighted Dusty for long walks and conned her cookery books, intent on finding recipes which were light on the housekeeping money.

It was about a week after she had left the hospital, and while she was rolling suet crust for the steak and kidney pudding she was making for supper that evening, when the door knocker was thumped smartly.

She dusted off floury hands and went to open the door, with the ridiculous hope that it might be connected in some way with the applications for work she had already sent. A geriatric hospital needed a part-time sister; a nursing home in Bishop's Stortford required someone to deputise for Matron, hours not specified; and a factory in Stevenage was asking for a nurse for the casualty department. She had applied to them all.

She opened the door and found herself confronting Dr van der Linden's massive person.

'Oh—good morning.' She added idiotically, 'There's only me here.'

'Cooking?' He had not said good morning, or even hello. 'I dare say you have time enough for that now?'

Without waiting to be asked, he went past her into the hall and on into the kitchen.

'I'm busy.' She shut the door and followed him there, and to add weight to her remark took up the rolling pin.

He sat down in the chair by the Aga, and Dusty spread himself over his feet. Louise rolled her pastry into a neat round. 'You may as well know,' she announced matter-of-factly, 'I've been made redundant. I finished last week.'

'I know. I'm on the hospital committee.' He ignored her gasp of surprise. 'Have you found anything else? There hasn't been much time, has there?'

'I have applied for several jobs; there hasn't been time for answers yet.' She laid her crust carefully over the pudding basin, made a small split in the centre, covered it with foil and fastened it with a rubber band, all the while not looking at him.

'Not panicking?' he asked casually.

'Certainly not.' She uttered the fib in what she hoped

was a confident voice. Of course she was panicking; nursing staff were being cut all over the country; she would be lucky to get a post locally.

She tidied away her cooking tools and asked politely, 'Would you like a cup of coffee?' She sought for another topic of conversation; she had no idea why he had come to see her, and there was something about his manner which made her uneasy. 'Mike and Christine are very happy at school,' she began chattily, 'and Zoë loves her job. She's joined the tennis club . . .'

'Yes, I know.' He sounded amused and she went pink; of course, Zoë would have told him . . .

She busied herself making coffee and, having poured it, sat down composedly at the kitchen table with her mug in front of her.

'Are you wondering why I came?' asked the doctor blandly.

'Yes.'

'I have a job for you—temporary but immediate. I have consulting rooms in Wimpole Street. I employ a receptionist and a nurse, who has unfortunately contracted jaundice; she will be away for several weeks, and in the meantime chaos reigns. Would you help out? I can't promise transport every day, for I quite often spend a night at the flat in town, but the hours are very easy, ten o'clock until four in the afternoon on weekdays. Occasionally I should need you for some special case—a private patient in his or her own home who may need nursing attention during an examination. I go abroad from time to time and usually take my nurse with me; since she is unable to accompany me you would have to take her place. Your salary would be the same as you have been receiving in hospital.'

'Ten o'clock until four five days a week is thirty hours—I work thirty-seven and a half; you would be paying me too much.'

'Oh, no. You will probably have less time for lunch, possibly no lunch at all at times, and the hours could vary.'

She was tempted to say yes at once; it was a heaven-sent chance to have a change, which might never come her way again. She might not hear from any of the jobs she had applied for, on the other hand one of them might turn out to be satisfyingly permanent and safe, whereas he had said that his offer was a temporary one. He got to his feet while she was pondering the question.

'Well, think about it and let me know,' he said easily. 'If you do decide to help me out, I'll pick you up tomorrow morning; I have to go to St Nicholas's first, but I can drop you off at my rooms and Miss Squires can show you round.'

He went unhurriedly to the door. 'Give me a ring around tea time, one way or the other,' he suggested, and before she could answer him he was in the hall and out of the front door.

After he had gone, she sat down and had another mug of coffee; now that the surprise of his offer had subsided a bit she felt a pleasant sense of excitement. She loved her work as a hospital sister, but just lately she had been conscious of a vague discontent. She had ignored it because she was sensible enough to know that to acknowledge it would be both useless and a waste of time. In a few more years Christine would be either trained or training for whatever she chose to do, Mike would be almost ready for university and, as for

Zoë, she would be married. To Aldo? Louise frowned suddenly. Zoë had a good deal to say about this young man at the office, a junior partner already, but would he be good enough for Zoë? She deserved the very best . . . Aldo, for instance, who appeared to have everything: good looks, charm when he chose to exert himself to use it, a lovely home, a splendid car, a more than comfortable income, and last but by no means least a growing reputation in his profession.

Louise offered Dusty a biscuit. 'It might be a good idea,' she told him. 'I'll get to know a bit more about him, I know it's not me he's interested in, but if I let him see that I approve of him wanting to marry Zoe . . . No, that won't do, much he cares about what anyone thinks if he has set his mind on something.' She drank the rest of her cold coffee. 'All the same, we need the money and it would give me a week or two to look for something permanent.'

Dusty barked his agreement, ate another biscuit and disposed himself for a nap.

Zoë was the last to get home; Louise waited for her before telling them her news. They received it with lively interest and a good deal of ill-concealed relief. 'Ring him up now, Louise,' begged Christine, 'otherwise he may think you don't want the job and find someone else.'

The doctor's calm acceptance vexed her; he sounded as though he had been sure she would accept without a second thought, and just for a moment she hesitated when he told her to be ready promptly in the morning; it was disconcerting, therefore, when the quiet voice in her ear said, 'No, don't change your mind, Louise. I'm depending on you.'

She said quietly, 'I'll be ready, and thank you, Aldo.'

She hung up and turned to face the three puzzled faces.

'Don't you like Aldo?' asked Christine. 'You sounded quite—well, icy.' She added, 'We all like him. If I were old enough, I'd like to marry him. Mike likes him, too, and Zoë dotes on him, don't you, Zoë?'

'Oh, rather, he is dreamy; I wouldn't mind being in your shoes, Louise.'

Probably, she thought, he wished the same thing; out loud she said, 'I do like him, you know, only I don't know him as well as you do. It's certainly a piece of luck that he needs a nurse; it'll give me time to find something permanent. The pay is the same, too.'

She was up in the morning betimes, anxious to be ready and waiting when the doctor called for her. The others were up, too, and crowded to the door to bid him a cheerful good morning and wish her luck.

Louise gave a final wave and settled back in her seat. 'I hope Dusty will be all right; Mike will take him out before he goes to school, and I'll be back before five o'clock. Christine ought to be home before then . . .'

She sounded worried, speaking her thoughts out loud, and the doctor gave her a quick sideways glance. 'Ah, I should have thought about that.' He slowed the car and reached for the phone between them. 'Potts, will you send Tim over to Ivy Cottage right away and tell him to arrange with Miss Zoë, or whoever is there, to take out Dusty at midday or thereabouts. He had better go right now before they leave for school. Thanks.'

He put back the receiver and picked up speed again. 'That will serve until we can think of something better.

Do you suppose that Zoë could take a longer lunch hour and go home and see to Dusty? If the buses fitted in—it's only four miles. How long does she get?'

'An hour. I believe that there are buses to fit it. Thank you for arranging for Tim to go over to the cottage—I should have done something about it.'

'You have hardly had the time. I go to Stevenage on Tuesdays or Wednesdays—I'll collect Zoë on my way and drop her off; it's no distance and I don't have a round until two o'clock; I can drive her back before I get to the hospital.'

'I'll talk to her about it this evening.' Louise sounded vexed and she was, but with herself. It was unlike her not to have everything planned and running smoothly; she must be losing her grip.

They were on the outskirts of London by now, the rows of dull brick houses gradually giving way to solidly built Victorian houses, and then streets of elegant Georgian terraces, immaculate and presenting dignified fronts to the outside world, concealing an equally dignified splendour within. Wimpole Street was almost empty of traffic. The doctor stopped half-way down it, got out, ushered Louise from the car and unlocked the elegant door of one of these houses. There were several brass plates beside it, but Louise was given no time to look at them; she was swept into a narrow hall, richly carpeted and pleasantly warm. There was a staircase to one side and another door beside it. The doctor opened this one, too, and urged her briskly forward. There were several doors in the square hall; he opened the first of them and then stood aside for her to go in.

The waiting-room was furnished in so restful a

manner that even the most nervous of patients would relax. There were small easy chairs dotted around, magazines on tables, vases of flowers, and in one corner a desk behind which sat an elderly lady: extremely thin, with a sharp nose and an old-fashioned hairdo. She had a pleasant face, despite the nose, and now she smiled warmly and got to her feet.

'Here she is, Miss Squires,' said the doctor. 'Louise Payne, come to help us out.' He watched them shake hands before going to the door. 'I have to be at St Nicholas's, so I must leave you to show her round; I haven't any patients until the afternoon, have I?'

'Two o'clock, Doctor,' said Miss Squires in a no-nonsense voice, 'and I've added two more to the list. You will have a busy afternoon.'

He nodded, gave Louise an encouraging smile and went away.

'We'll have a nice cup of tea,' declared Miss Squires, 'and get to know each other—that will be nice—and then I'll take you round. Mrs Pratt, the nurse, you know, left everything in apple-pie order. Terribly upset, she was, having to take sick leave, but the doctor has promised that she shall have her job back just as soon as she is quite fit.' She gave Louise a questioning look which Louise saw.

'Yes, he did explain that to me. I'm looking for a permanent job myself. I've always worked in a hospital—I hope I'll be able to cope here . . .'

Miss Squires was putting cups and saucers on a tray. 'Of course you will. It's very undemanding, no rush and hurry like hospitals, only occasionally he sees patients in the evening and visits them in their homes, too; that's when he takes you along; been abroad once or twice, too. He lectures a good deal . . . Come through here and see our little kitchen.'

A tiny cubicle, but well equipped for making tea and coffee and even a light meal. 'There is a daily woman who comes in to clean, but you look after the consulting room and the examination room next to it.'

She put on the kettle and then led the way into a large room at the back of the house, furnished in neutral colours, but with some good pictures and more flowers. The examination room was small, but had everything necessary in it, and beyond that was a small office which she was to use as her headquarters.

'Everything that you need is here,' said Miss Squires. 'Presently I will leave you to poke around. There is an overall behind the door: the doctor asked me to get it. I only hope he got the size right.' She measured Louise's person with her eyes. 'It looks to me as though he did.'

Louise hadn't said much; there hadn't been much chance, for Miss Squires was a good talker. Besides, there wasn't much need; she felt pretty sure that she would be able to manage once she had had the chance to see where everything was. 'The patients who are coming this afternoon?' she asked. 'May I see their notes?'

'Yes, of course. We'll have our tea and then feel free to do whatever you want. You know the hours? Ten o'clock until four, but it is often later, I warn you. Can you get to and fro easily?'

'Oh, yes, no problem. Dr van der Linden brought me this morning, but there's a good train service, and there is a tube close by, isn't there?'

'Very handy,' commented her companion, and poured the tea. 'Now do tell me something about yourself—the doctor said that you lived near him and had a sister—two sisters—and a brother, all younger?'

They spent a pleasant ten minutes or so before Miss Squires went back to her desk and Louise sat down to read the patients' notes, and by the time she had done that Miss Squires declared herself ready to go to lunch.

'I wasn't sure about my lunch hour,' said Louise. 'I brought sandwiches with me . . . Is there a place near here for coffee and a roll?'

Miss Squires nodded. 'Yes, and not too pricey, but you bring your lunch with you if you like. The place will be empty and you can make tea or coffee. I'll be back at half-past one.' Which gave Louise time to explore the whole place in peace.

She had her head buried in a cupboard, examining the various forms tidily arranged in it, when she heard the door to the waiting-room open.

'I'm here,' she called without looking round. 'I can't find the appointment cards and he'll be here any minute.'

'He's here now,' said Dr van der Linden into her ear, so that she spun round in a fine state of surprise. 'The cards are at the back of the second shelf on the left-hand side.'

'Heavens, you gave me a fright,' said Louise tartly. 'It's bad for anyone to be shocked like that.'

He eyed her pink cheeks, smiling slowly. 'But it suits you, Louise.'

Under his gaze her cheeks became even pinker. It really would not do, she told herself firmly, to feel like this just because Aldo had surprised her; so excited and delighted at the sight of him. He was going to be her brother-in-law, wasn't he? So she must cultivate a sisterly feeling towards him, not this pleasant glow spreading into her ribs.

He moved away and she closed the cupboard door, and was glad when Miss Squires joined them with the afternoon's appointments in one hand and a handful of telephone messages in the other.

Louise was kept busy for the entire afternoon. The patients who came were mostly elderly, several of them for the first time and apprehensive. Louise slid into her new role without difficulty; after running a busy ward it was positively restful, although at the end of the afternoon Miss Squires remarked that it had been a nice quiet beginning for her.

'You managed very well,' she observed kindly. 'Of course, Dr van der Linden is very easy to work for; very calm and good-natured and not easily put out. Of course, you worked for him at St Nicholas's, didn't you?'

'Well, not exactly for him,' said Louise, 'but I saw him frequently when I was Night Sister.'

They had tidied the room between them and were preparing to leave. The doctor had gone with a friendly nod and a word of thanks, and Louise cast a quick look at the clock on the waiting-room wall. It was only a little past half-past four; if she didn't have to hang around for a train she would be home by the time she had expected. Perhaps it would be quicker to get to the station by tube. She followed Miss Squires to the door, which was opened before they reached it.

'Ready?' asked the doctor, and looked at Louise. 'I'm going home, I'll drop you off. And you, Miss Squires.'

Louise got into the back of the car, with Miss Squires in the front, but when presently that lady got out in order to take the underground home, the doctor said over his shoulder, 'I have to go to St Nicholas's for a few minutes,' and without waiting for her reply wormed the car back into the beginnings of the rush-hour traffic.

At the hospital, he got out and opened her door. 'Get in front, Louise. I shan't be long.'

He was as good as his word; he was back within ten minutes and once more joined the stream of traffic outside the hospital forecourt. He didn't speak and neither did Louise, largely because she could think of nothing much to say. Besides, she was struggling to feel like a prospective sister-in-law; more difficult than she had thought it would be.

The traffic was thinning a little before the doctor spoke.

'Well, did you enjoy your first day?'

'Oh, yes. Very much. Miss Squires is a dear, isn't she? She took care that I did the right thing, and I hope that I did. It's quite different from the wards, though.'

'Indeed, yes. Far fewer patients, but none the less in need of help.'

She relaxed; this was safe ground upon which to hold a conversation. 'Do you have many private patients?'

'Yes, and quite a few of them away from London. I'm travelling up to Scotland next week, and I shall want you to come with me.'

'Oh—to stay? For how long?'

'One night, perhaps two. My patient is a charming old man who lives in a remote mansion. Too ill to make the journey down here. Remind me to give you the details tomorrow.'

'Yes, but what about Zoë and . . .'

'Would you agree to Miss Wills spending the night at Ivy Cottage? She could see to Dusty and make sure that everyone got off in the morning.'

'Well, yes . . .' She sounded hesitant and he added, 'She will have no objection. Indeed, I understand that she isn't too happy living with her sister.'

'How do you know that she won't mind?'

'I asked her.' She heard the amusement in his voice and bristled.

'You arranged it all behind my back! I'm not sure that I want to go to Scotland. Zoë and the others have never been on their own.'

'Zoë is quite old enough to cope, surely? I have had the impression that she would be capable of running a household easily enough.'

A remark which brought her up short; it would never do to sow the seeds of doubt in his mind about Zoe's capabilities. Even if he were head over heels in love with her, he would want a wife capable of running his home and entertaining his guests.

'Zoë is very capable,' she said stiffly.

'She can always call upon Miss Wills if she gets worried about anything. Besides, we shall drive up on Sunday and they will all be at home.' He eased the car past a bulk carrier; they were almost at Much Hadham. 'You will come?' It sounded more like a statement than a question.

'Very well.' She felt the surge of excitement again, although her voice was as serene as it usually was.

'Good; I'll fill you in tomorrow. I shall be at Stevenage, so Zoë will be able to go home at lunch time—I'll pick her up and take her back to the office. I'll be in just after two o'clock and we may be working late.

I'll take you back with me—it will be some time after six o'clock, I should imagine.'

He turned his head to look at her in the dimness of the car. 'It must seem disorganised to you after working in hospital.'

'Well, yes, but it makes a change and I think I shall enjoy it, and I'm very grateful . . .'

He cut her short. 'I'm the one who is grateful.' He slowed as they reached the village, and stopped before her door which was instantly flung open as her sisters and brother surged out, Dusty barking at their heels.

'Louise, there you are!' exclaimed Zoë, uttering the obvious. 'And Aldo—come in and have a cup of coffee?'

He shook his head, smiling down at her. 'No time. Ask me again some time. Louise will tell you what we have arranged for tomorrow. I'll fetch you from the office—you get an hour from twelve-thirty, don't you?—bring you here so that you can see to Dusty, and pick you up again to drive you back. Louise will explain what we have in mind.' He got back into the car after a few words with Mike and Christine, nodded casually to Louise and drove away.

Louise was borne inside and presently they all sat down to supper, a meal which went on for some time since there was so much to talk about. When the younger ones had gone to bed, Louise explained abut the plans she and Aldo had made for Zoë. 'If you could arrange something, love,' begged Louise. 'Dusty will be all right if you could manage to get here for lunch each day, take him for a ten-minute trot and get a bus back. Aldo says that he will drive you to and fro when he goes to Stevenage, so that only leaves four days. If it's impossible, he suggested that Miss Wills might help out.'

'Not to worry,' declared Zoë 'I'm sure they won't mind at the office. I'm not all that important you know. I'll fix something up tomorrow. Did you really like your day working for Aldo?'

'Oh, yes. Of course, it's not like ward work, but I've always liked working for him; he is very calm and unhurried, you know and I'm so used to his ways.'

Zoë got up to put on the kettle for a last cup of tea before bed. 'It's funny, you only know him as a consultant, and I suppose that carries a kind of aura, but I've never seen him being a doctor. He's just a very attractive man to me, and great fun to be with.'

Louise fetched the tea-tray. She thought a little wistfully that very likely he was, but it seemed unlikely that she would ever get more than a glimpse of that side of him. She said matter-of-factly, 'I dare say he is. His patients like him.'

She was up betimes in the morning to catch the train and then get a bus to Wimpole Street. Miss Squires had just arrived and was busy sorting the post. She bade Louise good morning and continued, 'Such a lot of invitations the doctor gets, you would have no idea . . . Very much in demand he is, socially. Him not being married and so handsome. He refuses most of them; he has got a number of friends though, but that is to be expected, isn't it? Amazing that some woman hasn't caught his eye. I asked him one day why he didn't marry, and do you know what he said? "If I can't find my dream girl, I'll stay single." Of course, I've worked for him for so long, he doesn't mind what he says to me.' She went on in a severe voice, 'Of course, he's not one to talk about himself.'

When Louise said warmly, 'No, I am sure he's not,' she added,

'You're a sensible girl, I can see that, and not one to gossip.'

They went about their various chores then, stopping for coffee, and presently they were ready for the afternoon's work. Miss Squires went out for lunch and Louise retired to the kitchen and made a pot of tea to wash down her sandwiches . . .

Dr van der Linden arrived when he'd said he would, and ten minutes later came the first of his patients, a crusty old man, wheezing his way into the consulting room with chronic bronchitis. He was irritable and impatient, but the doctor dealt with him gently and Louise, taking her cue from him, met the old man's crustiness with a serenity which remained untroubled by his ill humour. As she showed him out at length, he paused at the door.

'You are a sensible young woman, no flummery about you—can't bear flummery.'

The next patient was one she recognised at once: Mr Tom Cowdrie, accompanied by his wife. He had come for a check-up, and Louise was surprised to see Mrs Cowdrie with him. There she was, fussing round him in a devoted wifely way, the very antithesis of her former behaviour at St Nicholas's. She was beautifully dressed and exquisitely made-up and overflowing with charm. Louise, who hadn't liked her when they had first met, disliked her more now.

She insisted on going into the consulting room with her husband, and Louise, standing discreetly in the background, watched her get to work upon the doctor, who greeted her with suave politeness and then turned his attention to his patient, affording Louise a good deal of satisfaction; it annoyed Mrs Cowdrie, but her best efforts made no impression on his bland manner. Louise showed them out with a deep sense of complacency.

The patient who followed was a different kettle of fish; a small, elderly lady, dressed with elegant shabbiness, who thanked Louise nicely as she was ushered in and advanced with outstretched hand to greet the doctor. She had a heart condition which was not going to get any better, and the doctor treated her gently, at the same time matching her matter-of-fact manner with his own. When she had gone and Louise had gone back to the examination room to tidy it, he looked up from his desk to say, 'A brave little lady. I wish I could do more for her. Is there time for a cup of tea before the next patient?' He glanced at the list Miss Squires had put on his desk. 'You won't mind staying on after four o'clock?'

'Not in the least, Doctor. I'll get your tea.'

He was writing when she went back, and she saw that he was preoccupied so she said nothing, but whisked herself away to share the teapot with Miss Squires before the next patient arrived.

It was almost six o'clock when the last patient was ushered out. Louise tidied up briskly, but all the same the doctor was waiting for her when she emerged from the cloakroom ready to go home. Miss Squires had already left, and Louise muttered an apology as she nipped round closing doors and switching off the lights. As they got into the car he said, 'I'll be at St Nicholas's in the morning, so I can drive you here—be ready by eight-thirty, will you? I've only three or four patients for tomorrow afternoon, so you should be able to get away on time. Are the trains convenient?'

Even if they hadn't been she would have said yes.

He said in his calm way, 'Now, about Scotland. We will drive up on Sunday, leaving early—seven o'clock. We can stop for breakfast on the way, and with another stop for lunch we should be at Dirleton round about tea time. I'll see my patient on Monday morning, and confer with his doctor, and then I shall need to talk to him; I doubt if we will leave that day. If possible I should like to leave after breakfast on Tuesday, and we will be back here the same evening, for I have a round at Stevenage on Wednesday morning.'

Louise digested this with her usual serenity. 'Where is Dirleton?' was her only response.

'On the Firth of Forth, about half an hour's drive from Edinburgh. It's on the south shore of the Firth. We stay the night at my patient's house.'

'You would like me to wear uniform?'

'Please. My patient is bedridden; at present his wife and daughter manage, but he will need a nurse, although I believe he doesn't want that.' He glanced at her. 'Understood?'

'Yes, thank you. Am I to know more about your patient before I meet him?'

'I'll give you the notes to read tomorrow.'

He drove in silence after that until he stopped at Ivy Cottage. It had been like doing a ward round in a car, thought Louise, bidding him a sedate goodnight.

'Don't keep me waiting in the morning.' He drove off with the briefest of goodnights.

She went into the house and found everyone in the

kitchen getting supper. Zoë looked up from the eggs she was beating. 'Hello, Louise—did Aldo bring you back? Didn't he want to come in? He stayed for a cup of coffee when he brought me back for lunch—he is such fun, isn't he?'

Obviously that had something to do with the person he was with, thought Louise, and she smiled in what she hoped looked like agreement.

'I fixed up my lunch hour—no problems, the buses fit in beautifully; I'll have time to take Dusty for a walk.' She eyed Louise. 'Are you tired?'

Christine, setting knives and forks on the table, chimed in, 'Of course she's tired. I'll make a pot of tea while supper is cooking.'

Over supper, Louise explained about going to Scotland. 'I'll be away for two days and two nights; it's miles away, isn't it? Dr—that is, Aldo suggested that Miss Wills might come each day and see to things. Do you think that is a good idea? She will sleep here, too; it seems she's not too happy with her sister. She can have my room.'

Zoë looked pleased. 'Do you suppose she would? I could go to the tennis club on Monday evening if she was here . . . Is Aldo going to arrange it for us?'

'Good heavens, he won't want to be bothered with our piffling arrangements, I'll go and see her tomorrow evening.'

'Well, I don't see why he wouldn't want to. After all, he does keep an eye on us, doesn't he? Like a nice big brother—or even a husband or boyfriend.' Christine spoke reflectively.

'Whose husband?' asked Mike, and leaned across the table to tug at her hair. 'You're only a kid, and Zoë's too mooney and Louise wouldn't want to marry him, would you, Louise?'

His eldest sister poured herself another cup of tea before she answered him. 'It's a hypothetical question, isn't it?' Her voice was as quiet and sensible as it always was, while somewhere deep inside her an insistent voice was telling her that there was nothing she would like better than to marry Aldo. With the blinding clarity of hindsight, she knew that she had been in love with him for a long time without ever allowing herself to acknowledge it. So very unfortunate when he regarded her as a useful nurse who happened to be needing a job when he had one to offer and, moreover, was Zoë's elder sister.

She said cheerfully, 'I've enough on my plate with you lot—a husband would be the last straw!' And she reflected wryly that she would have to cultivate a sisterly affection for Aldo; if she started now, this very minute, it might be possible.

Towards the end of a wakeful night, she knew it wasn't going to be possible. Instead it was going to be awkward, but she had been dealing with awkward situations for some years now and she was quite good at them. Somehow or other she would have to maintain the pleasant, rather stand-offish relationship she had had with Aldo, and never, never let him guess that she loved him.

She rolled over in bed and buried her head in the pillow. It would be difficult, but she had always accepted a challenge. She slept on this uplifting thought.

CHAPTER SIX

LOUISE awoke with the soothing thought that it was Friday; on Saturday there were no patients and there would be no need to see Aldo. As for today, she was quite sure that she would be able to maintain her habitual calm in his company. She didn't feel quite so sure as she got into the Jaguar beside him, but by dint of not looking at him and enthusing about the delightful weather she prided herself on doing rather well, despite the fact that her heart was thumping like a mad thing and her cheeks were rather pinker than usual.

The doctor, an observant man, smiled to himself and encouraged her to enthuse about the bright morning; he was a man of infinite patience, prepared to wait for what he wanted. At his rooms he gave her the notes on the old gentleman he was going to see, saying easily, 'We can discuss the case as we go. I have no spare time today.'

Which was true enough; there were more patients than usual, and he went to St Nicholas's too, telephoning just before four o'clock to tell her that he would not be able to drive her back to Much Hadham.

When Louise told Miss Squires, that lady said comfortably, 'He's a very careful man, takes great care of his patients—someone very ill, I dare say. Anyway, he had an invitation for this evening—some dinner party or other in Sloane Square.'

She began to tidy her desk. 'If you get straight, there's no reason why we shouldn't leave on time. I'll set the answering machine. You will need a nice quiet day tomorrow, ready for Sunday; the doctor doesn't spare himself, so I warn you. Mrs Pratt got exhausted. He tends to drive for hours, you know.'

'Thanks for warning me,' said Louise. She didn't think she would mind that, even if he didn't speak to her, or forgot she was there; it wouldn't matter. She would be sitting beside him, watching his large, capable hands on the wheel. Never mind the problematical future, she reflected, the present would do very nicely for the moment.

On Sunday she was ready by a quarter to seven. The other three were in dressing-gowns, hovering around her as though she were off to the ends of the earth. She had packed a small case with two clean overalls, her navy belt with the silver buckle, black stockings and sensible duty shoes and, urged by both her sisters, was wearing a cotton jersey skirt and blouse with their matching jacket, an outfit she had bought the previous year and seldom worn. It was a soft blue and, as they pointed out to her, wouldn't crush if she had to sit still for hours on end. Never mind if she had intended to keep it for special occasions; if this wasn't a special occasion, said Christine forcefully, she would like to know what was.

They crowded to the door as the Jaguar drew up, and amid a welter of good mornings to Aldo, goodbyes to herself and a string of reassurances as to how they would manage without her, Louise got into the car.

The doctor gave her a little nod and an approving glance. She looked very pretty; she also looked nicely dressed in an understated way and as neat as a new pin, and perfectly composed. He gave a final wave to the group in the doorway and started the car. Louise turned to wave, too, but she did not speak; she was full to the brim with excitement and happiness, but they were well hidden. To her companion this was all part of his work; probably he would spend most of the long journey mulling over his patient's prospects.

It seemed that that might be so, for he didn't speak for quite a time. They had driven across country to join the main road to Royston, and then the long stretch to Huntingdon and the A1. Louise, aware of empty insides, thought that once they were on that, her companion would settle down to drive without stopping. He hadn't mentioned breakfast; he might have changed his mind about the plan to have it on the way and have had a meal before they left. Her cup of tea, taken at six o'clock, seemed a poor substitute.

They went through Huntingdon without pause and now the A1 was only a mile or so away, so it was with the greatest relief to her when he drew up smoothly before the Brampton Hotel. The town was still only half awake on a Sunday morning, but the place looked welcoming.

'Breakfast?' asked Louise hopefully.

The doctor's mouth twitched. 'Hungry? Good. Make a good meal, for we have a long stretch ahead of us.' With which ominous words he got out of the car and came to open her door for her and usher her into the hotel.

Louise paused inside the vestibule and the doctor said, 'Over there, behind those potted palms; I'll be in the breakfast room.' He added, 'We have half an hour.'

Louise didn't waste time on her face and hair; indeed, she still looked remarkably fresh and tidy. Hunger hurried her to the breakfast room where she found the doctor lounging at the table, reading *The Sunday Times*. He put it down as she joined him, and they sat down to a well-laden table. Twenty minutes later they rose from it, having eaten with good appetites, and Louise prudently disappeared behind the potted palms once more; the doctor had mentioned a long stretch; for all she knew they might not stop until they were in Scotland.

They were on the A1 now, making for Grantham and then Newark. The doctor, with the air of a man who was enjoying himself, talked of this and that in a casual fashion, so that presently Louise found that she was enjoying herself mightily; the journey was taking on the air of a day's outing. No mention had been made of his patient, but there was time enough.

She asked, 'You've been this way before?'

'Several times. We should be at Scotch Corner in just under four hours from Much Hadham, and that includes the stop for breakfast. There is a stretch of motorway soon, but we rejoin the A1 again; we can stop for coffee at Wetherby.'

He glanced down at her. 'There's a road map in the pocket beside you . . .'

She was relieved to see that, at the rate they were travelling, coffee wasn't all that far off.

They stopped at Wetherby as Aldo had promised; the hotel was large and modern and the coffee was excellent. Much refreshed, she faced with equanimity · the prospect of the stretch ahead of them; Scotch Corner, she was told, then the motorway to Newcastle and pick up the A1 to the north of the city and on to Berwick-on-Tweed.

'Tired?' asked Aldo.

She answered with perfect truth that she wasn't. 'This car is very comfortable,' she observed, 'and you drive very well—I mean, I'm not in the least nervous.'

He thanked her gravely and asked her if she drove herself.

'Well, years ago I did, but we sold the car . . . As soon as I can I will get Zoë to learn and get her a licence.'

He nodded. 'You're an exemplary elder sister, Louise.'

She flushed. 'That makes me sound like a frightful bossy prig.'

'The very last thing you are. Now, suppose that I fill you in about my patient?'

Which he did while the miles were left behind, and presently they were on the motorway with the city ahead of them. The traffic, even on a Sunday, was thick now, and she forebore from asking any more questions, although she thought that the doctor was perfectly capable of driving and answering her queries at the same time. Surely he must be feeling tired by now? It was after one o'clock and, according to the map, there was still a good distance to go.

'Lunch at Alnwick,' said Aldo, and put his foot down.

The hotel, when they reached it, was old but extremely comfortable. They lunched off game soup, hunter's chicken with buttered rice and *crème soufflé à l'orange* and drank tonic water since the doctor was driving and Louise had no wish to drink wine unless he did so. They didn't sit over their coffee; she was given ten minutes in which to put herself to rights then she was ushered back into the car, on what would be the last stage of their long journey.

They covered the thirty odd miles to Berwick-upon-Tweed in a little over half an hour, and then followed the coast until the road turned inward for a short distance, turning back again to the sea, but once through Dunbar the doctor turned off the A1 at last, following a road which twisted and turned until finally it brought to view a ruined castle perched on a hill.

'Dirleton,' said Aldo. He didn't sound in the least tired, and Louise, who had been fighting a strong desire to sleep for the last few miles, sat up straight to look.

The village was at the foot of the hill, its cottages encircling a green which led to the church. It looked delightful and she said so.

'Charming, isn't it?' he agreed. 'The shore isn't too far away. A pity there will be no time to explore.'

The house they were bound for was a little way out of the village; a grey stone edifice a good deal smaller than the vast mansion they could see in the distance, but none the less a building to command respect. It was approached through a small park shielded from the sea wind by a group of conifers. The doctor drew up on the sweep before the front door and got out. As he opened her door he said quietly, 'Don't be nervous. After we have seen the general you will be led away to your room; change into uniform if you will and then come downstairs again. I'll look out for you.'

The door opened as they approached it. The man standing there greeted them austerely; he was elderly, but his eyes were a bright blue and he held himself erect. The doctor addressed him easily and his stern features relaxed into a smile, but he didn't smile at Louise when the doctor introduced him to her, only gave her a long, considered look.

He led them through a chilly hall, its walls panelled with dark wood and ornamented with stuffed tigers' heads and any number of other creatures Louise couldn't put a name to. Sandwiched between these were lethal weapons, arranged artistically in squares and circles. She caught the doctor's eye and looked away quickly; he looked serious enough, but she thought that he was amused, probably at her. She walked beside him, very much on her dignity; love him she might, but that didn't prevent her finding him tiresome. Tiresome, she had to admit honestly, only because for half the time she had no idea what he was really thinking.

The room they entered was rather like the hall, but on a smaller scale, and had the benefit of a large fireplace in which burned a cheerful fire. There were one or two comfortable chairs, too, and from one of them rose a tall, thin lady, well past middle age, wearing a twin set and a tweed skirt, both of excellent quality but of no particular colour. She had a long face and a high-bridged nose, but her smile was charming.

'Dr van der Linden, what a pleasure to see you again, and you have brought your nurse with you . . .'

Louise was introduced and, after a brief murmur, retired a little behind the doctor's vast bulk until, the civilities done with, they were led across the room to a chair by the fire where the general sat. He was dozing, which gave her the chance to take stock of him. He was an ill man, congestive heart failure; she would have seen that for herself without the doctor's meticulous priming. He must have been a handsome man when he was young; even now, though he was old and ill, he had good looks, with white hair and a big moustache.

He opened his eyes suddenly, fixed her with a stare and barked in a wheezing voice, 'Who are you, miss? Haven't seen you before, have I?' He saw the doctor then. 'Ha, you're here. Man of your word, aren't you? Said you would be here for tea. I'm not in the mood to be mauled about this evening. Charles Donaldson will be here early tomorrow, you can put your heads together and go over me in the morning.' He added defiantly, 'I got out of my bed. Don't see why I shouldn't, do you, eh?'

The doctor agreed calmly, merely remarking that his nurse would need to deal with one or two trifling procedures that evening. 'Sister Payne is very efficient,' he added soothingly, 'and it will merely be a matter of a test or two.'

'Oh, well, I suppose you know what you are about,' conceded the general grumpily, and since he was short of breath he said no more.

'You would like tea?' asked his wife. 'But first I'll get someone to take Sister Payne to her room—such a long journey—you must be tired.'

An elderly maid led Louise upstairs and along a narrow corridor, to open a door at its end. The room was well furnished, but austere; there were no flowers and few ornaments, and the polished floor struck chill as she kicked off her shoes to ease her feet. But the view from the window was a delight; the castle, silhouetted against the early evening sky, was quite magnificent. She left the window presently, changed into her white overall, put on her sensible shoes and smoothed her hair under the cap she wore at the doctor's rooms, and then went downstairs.

The general's wife was sitting behind a small table in the drawing-room, pouring tea from a silver teapot into paper-thin cups. The same maid who had shown her to her room handed the cups and saucers, proffered small sandwiches and little cakes and then, at a word from her mistress, left the room. Louise exchanged small talk with the lady of the house while she watched the doctor, quite at his ease, making a good tea while listening to the general puffing and blowing his way through army reminiscences.

Presently the old man said, 'Dare say you would like a breath of fresh air after being in the car all day. You know your way around. Take a walk in the grounds. Perhaps Sister Payne would like to accompany you?'

So Louise found herself strolling along the wide paths behind the house, a shawl borrowed from her hostess around her shoulders, for the evening was cool, with the doctor beside her. They made a striking pair and, from a distance, romantic, too, only anyone near enough to listen to their conversation would have been disappointed to hear the doctor, in a dry-as-dust voice, discussing his patient with his companion, for all the world as though they were walking down the centre of a hospital ward instead of on a flower-bordered path with a charming vista ahead of them. Someone, a long time ago, had had the grounds laid out with an eye to making the most of the terrain. There was a small fountain at the end of the path and a grotto away to their left, reached by another path, and a miniature Greek temple on a gentle rise to their other side.

Louise, saying 'yes, certainly', and 'I quite understand', and, 'I'll see that it's done, Doctor', reflected that it was a terrible waste to carry on such a businesslike conversation in such surroundings.

'You're not listening to a word,' said Aldo mildly.

She said guiltily, 'Oh, I am. I know exactly what you want me to do . . .'

He said drily, 'The surroundings are hardly conducive to such dry talk. I believe that your head is full of roses and moonshine, and you are wondering about the men and women who may have walked here in more romantic circumstances.'

'Well, it is romantic, you know. Grottoes and things,' she added vaguely, and thought how wonderful it would be if he were to take her in his arms and kiss her, a hollow hope.

He turned her round smartly. 'In which case, I think it advisable not to visit the grotto.' A remark which made her face flame in the gathering dusk. Just in case he had thought that she was making a play for him, she became at once haughty and coldly polite. Detestable, horrible man; once back at home she would avoid him like the plague. Never, never, she promised herself, would he get the chance to say anything like that again. She shivered with her strong feelings, and he said at once, 'You're cold, we have stayed out too long.'

'It seemed a long time,' she agreed sweetly, and because of the gathering darkness didn't see his raised eyebrows and then his brief smile.

Dinner was eaten in some splendour in a gloomy dining-room furnished with beautifully polished dark oak, worn with age, but the table linen was crisply white and set with fine china and silver. The general, being on a diet, was inclined to be grumpy, but his wife and Aldo carried on a practised conversation born of coping with difficult situations. Not quite his bedside manner, reflected Louise, but something approaching it. It quite obviously soothed his somewhat irascible patient.

The general retired to bed presently, and after a suitable interval Louise went along to see to the various tasks the doctor had asked her to do. Pulse and blood pressure and temperature and respirations, an intake and output chart to cover twenty-four hours, a measured carafe of water set by the bedside and finally her firm request that it should be drained by eight o'clock in the morning.

'Been nursing long?' enquired the general. In bed now, he had relaxed and even looked good-natured.

'Years and years,' she told him, 'but almost always in hospital.'

'Ought to be married, a pretty girl like you.'

She smiled at him. 'You know, General, I've not had the time; my parents are dead and I have a younger brother and two sisters.'

The old man snorted. 'Don't tell me you are content with your lot.'

'Oh, but I am,' she assured him cheerfully, 'until circumstances change. They do, you know.'

'Mustn't discuss the doctor with you, I suppose?'

'I think not. I work for him, you see. Besides, I think he is a fine man and a splendid physician. Can I do anything more for you, General? Do you like to read for a while, or shall I turn off the lights?'

'I shall read for an hour or so. Besides I dare say van der Linden will be along presently.'

'Then I'll say goodnight.'

Outside on the wide corridor leading to the staircase she paused, wondering if she should go back downstairs or go straight to her room. She decided to go back to the drawing-room, wish her hostess goodnight and then go to bed.

The doctor got up as she went into the room, and the general's wife put down the needlework she was doing. 'I'll go and say goodnight,' she said, 'then you can go up presently, Doctor. The general sets great store by a visit from you.'

He held the door for her and closed it quietly behind her. 'Do sit down.' She did as he suggested. 'Did everything go well upstairs?'

Louise perched on the edge of a small upright chair. She said, 'Yes, thank you,' in a chilly voice and added, 'If there is nothing more for me to do, I'll go to bed.'

He said mildly, 'We have spent the whole of a long day in each other's company in unqualified amiablility, but I detect a certain frostiness in your manner, Louise. What have I done—or not done?'

She gave him a startled look. 'Done? I don't understand you.' She embarked on a string of remarks which became more and more tangled, while he sat quietly, watching her, saying nothing, but presently he took pity on her and said gravely, 'I dare say you are tired, Louise. I'll explain to our hostess when she returns, and bid her goodnight on your behalf.'

'I'm not tired,' began Louise, and then stopped when she saw him smile. 'Goodnight,' she said stonily, and made for the door. Not quite quickly enough; he was there before her, his hand on the doorhandle so that perforce she had to come to a halt.

He was much too close for her peace of mind. She caught her breath and steadied it deliberately, her eyes fixed on the massive chest before her. It would have been nice to lay her head upon it and have a good cry . . .

He said slowly, 'I asked you just now what I had done or not done. There was no need because I already know, Louise.' He paused and sighed. 'I did it deliberately, but this is neither the time nor the place to explain.'

'No need,' she told him, and now she was quite matter of fact, 'and I'm so sorry I was snappy. I think I am more tired than I realised.' She managed a quite normal smile. 'I did enjoy the drive, though.'

He had opened the door, and was looking down at her with an expression hard to read. 'So did I. Goodnight, Louise.' He sounded all of a sudden very austere.

She did not sleep well; she told herself it was the strange bedroom—chilly, she guessed, because it was seldom slept in. But it wasn't entirely due to her cold feet that she lay awake for such a long time; somehow, at some time, things had changed between Aldo and herself. It had been an effort to maintain the casual friendly attitude towards him once she had discovered that she was in love with him, but she had done her best for Zoë's sake; at all costs they must remain friends if she were to become his sister-in-law, but now she wasn't at all sure if he liked her. After all, she reasoned, until recently he had had no need to be more than polite when they met each other in the hospital; now he saw more of her he might not like her at all, even though he was in love with Zoë. She got out of bed and put on her dressing-gown and back she got in again, curling her feet into its warmth. Really, life was very strange; on the one hand good fortune had smiled on her, offering her Ivy Cottage and a little money in the bank so that Mike and Christine could go to decent schools and Zoë could have some fun, and then, just as she was feeling smug and secure, she had lost her job and, what was much worse, had fallen in love with Aldo, who was Zoë's . . .

She fell at last into a troubled sleep, to be wakened by the elderly maid with early-morning tea.

She got up at once and dressed; there were things to do for the general, and probably he would object to most of them.

The house was quiet as she went along the wide corridor to the front of the house. She was passing the head of the stairs when she glanced down and saw that the doctor was in the hall. He looked up and came up the stairs two at a time.

She had not expected to see him, although she had been thinking about him from the moment she opened her eyes, so that the colour rushed into her face and she stammered a little as she wished him good morning.

He stood looking at her, his own greeting laconic, although his eyes had missed nothing. 'You slept well? Your room is at the back, isn't it? Mine is at the other end of the corridor; if I had wanted your help in an emergency it would have been a day's march to reach you!'

Louise chuckled, just for a moment forgetting her mixed-up feelings.

'That's better, you looked as though you were carrying the world's cares on your shoulders. ' And, at her look, 'You see, last time I came here for a consultation, I had Mrs Pratt with me; middle-aged and businesslike and motherly; you are far too pretty for the job, Louise.' He stared at her thoughtfully. 'I'm wrong, you're not pretty, you're beautiful.'

Before she could close her astonished mouth to ask him if he had lost his wits, he had gone, walking rapidly away towards his room without looking back.

Not a good start to the day, thought Louise, her feelings now in such a turmoil, she had no idea how to sort them out. Common sense prevailed. She tapped on the general's door and went in, looking efficient and serene and capable of dealing with any situation which might arise.

The general disapproved of illness, his own most of all. He had a theory that if one ignored whatever it was that was wrong with one, it would go away. He explained this at some length to Louise, so that time was lost before she could cajole him into allowing her to take his temperature and pulse, and his blood pressure, and check that he had drunk his carafe of water. She was quite surprised to find that he had.

She adjourned to the bathroom to make the few simple tests the doctor needed, listened with sympathy to his grumbles about the miserable diet he was forced to endure and presently went down to her breakfast. The family doctor would be arriving shortly; she didn't suppose that she would be required to attend the consultation, but she would have to remain within calling distance in order to iron out any little problems the learned gentlemen might have, take notes, find things for them and probably pour their coffee. Later she would have to be in attendance while they examined their patient.

The elderly man who had opened the door to them was in the hall. His good morning was uttered gloomily, but she guessed that that was his normal expression. He led her to a small room at the back of the hall where breakfast had been laid. There was no one there and she sat down with a sigh of relief, for she didn't want to meet Aldo for a little while, not until she had regained her habitual calm. She had allowed her love to cloud her common sense. He had been joking; perhaps he felt that she needed cheering up . . .

She accepted coffee from the butler, took a boiled egg from the dish he offered her and began on her solitary meal. She had almost finished when the doctor joined her, and with a brief smile sat down to his own coffee and eggs. 'You've seen the general?' he wanted to know. 'What do you think of him? Give me some kind of report, will you, before I go and see him?'

Which made it quite easy, after all, for she slipped back into impersonal professionalism without effort.

He nodded when she had finished. 'Dr Donaldson will be here directly; we'll have a chat and then see the general. I shall want you there. After lunch an ambulance will take him into Edinburgh to be X-rayed; you will go with him and remain with him. I'll be there, too, of course. Dr Donaldson will come back later today, and we will discuss what's best to be done. We will leave after breakfast in the morning.'

Louise said, 'Very well,' in a composed voice, and then, 'You will excuse me if I go, there are one or two things . . .'

He said blandly, 'I thought there might be.' A remark which she viewed with suspicion.

In fact, there was nothing for her to do; the general had refused her services in a whispered roar. 'Can't stop you taking temperatures and so on, but I'm damned if you are going to wash me, Miss . . . What's your name?'

'Louise, General. All right, I won't wash you.' She smiled at him. 'But I will have to be here with the doctors—to turn back bedcovers and hand them things and help them generally. You won't mind that?'

He actually chuckled. 'A pretty girl like you? Shan't mind at all.'

Presently she went downstairs to be introduced to Dr Donaldson, who was youngish, rugged featured and a little in awe of Dr van der Linden; she left them together and went to sit with her hostess in the drawing-room, carrying on a light conversation calculated to keep that lady's mind occupied with anything but her husband's condition. It was gone eleven o'clock before she was summoned to go upstairs to the general's room, where the two doctors carried out a lengthy examination.

Louise, standing out of the way, felt a flow of pleasure at the way Aldo treated both his patient and Dr Donaldson, his manner exactly right: relaxed—modest, she reflected, was the right word—and yet full of assurance. She remained behind when they at last left their patient, tidied the bed, recommended that he should remain in bed for his lunch and, when he protested, pointed out that the afternoon would be rather tiring.

'You will come with me?'

'Yes, Dr van der Linden has asked me to do so.'

'Like working for him?'

'Yes, very much.' She willed herself not to blush, but did, to her annoyance.

When she went downstairs again the two doctors were still conferring, but very shortly Dr Donaldson wen away with the promise to return after the general was back from Edinburgh, and Aldo went to talk to his wife.

Louise, with nothing to do for the moment, wandered outside on to the terrace and sat down on the wall separating it from the lawns below. She would have liked to have explored, but she didn't dare go far from the house in case she was needed. After lunch she would have to oversee her patient's passage to the ambulance and go with him to the hospital. Aldo would be there, but even if she saw him there it would be in a professional capacity, and Dr Donaldson would be back in the evening and probably stay for a time. Tomorrow she would be with Aldo all day . . .

She became aware that he was standing beside her and she got to her feet. 'You wanted me for something?'

He shook his head. 'Sit down again, Louise,' and, when she did, he sat beside her. 'The general's condition has worsened since I saw him last. I've changed his drugs and agreed on his treatment with Donaldson. I've talked to his wife, too. There is really very little that I can do, I'm afraid; they are both aware of that. Donaldson is a good chap and the general is in good hands. He will be tired by the time he gets back here; you'll see him into his bed and comfortable, I know—he has taken a fancy to you. He will have to have a nurse in the house; I've promised to see if the hospital can lend him one as pretty as you—his words, not mine.'

Louise's charming bosom swelled with indignation; she had been listening to him with increasing sympathy and interest, and he had to spoil it all. Perhaps he wanted to make sure that she hadn't taken him seriously yesterday evening . . . Well, she hadn't and she never would.

She said, 'How kind of him. I'm sure you will find someone. He really does need a nurse. I like him.'

'So do I. You're not sorry you came?'

'Me? No, why should I be? I haven't had much to do, though.'

'You've been my right hand.'

The afternoon went off well. True, the drive in the ambulance was tiring, partly because the general had become peevish and it took all Louise's skill to prevent him bursting out into a rage, something which would have done him no good at all.

He was too tired to be cross by the time they got back. Louise saw him back into his bed, sat him against his pillows and gave him oxygen until he had settled down. Aldo, coming quietly into the room, sat himself down by the bed and explained the results of the X-rays to his patient. 'They could be worse,' he told him in his level and unhurried voice, 'and we can prevent that happening . . . Sister, I'm sure you would like a cup of tea.' His voice was smoothly firm. 'The general and I are going to have a talk.'

'You'll let me know when you want me back, sir?' She was at the door already; she could take a hint as well as the next one.

Tea had been set for her in a little room she had not been into before. There was no one about, but the teapot was hot under its cosy and there were scones and buttered toast. She eased her tired feet from their shoes and sat down.

They left soon after eight o'clock the next morning; Dr Donaldson had been back during the evening, and when he had gone Aldo went back to talk to the general again. When she had said goodbye to him just before they left he had taken her hand and wheezed quite cheerfully, 'Always feel better when van der Linden has been. Good chap he is, trust him—believe him, too. So does my wife.' He patted her hand. 'See that he brings you with him when he comes next time.'

She smiled at him, for she liked him, and she admired his peppery courage. His wife had come to the door to see them off. 'Thank you for coming, Dr van der Linden. You have no idea how much easier we feel now that you have seen my husband again.'

He took her hand and shook it gently. 'The general is holding his own and Dr Donaldson will keep him to it. He will get in touch with me if he thinks it necessary.'

He waited while Louise was thanked, and smiled a little when she was bidden to return next time the doctor came. 'For the general likes you, my dear.'

Louise got into the car, murmuring politely, and a moment later Aldo was beside her and they had started their journey home. The whole day before them, she thought, and even if Aldo wasn't inclined to be friendly he would be there beside her. The journey up to Scotland had been delightful; who knew if the return might not be even better?

CHAPTER SEVEN

IT WAS a grey morning and chilly, with a strong wind blowing in from the sea, but the car was warm and Louise settled into the comfortable seat and sat silent. Aldo had nothing to say for a time, and she contented herself with looking at the country around them until he spoke finally.

'There's a good B road from Grantshouse—it will take us eventually to Kelso—we go through Duns and Preston—nice border country.'

Louise was peering at the map, glad that he had broken a silence which had gone on for too long. 'And where do we go from there?'

'Jedburgh—we'll have coffee there, bypass Otterburn on the A68 to Darlington and after that on to the A1. We might lunch somewhere around there—it is round about two hundred and fifty miles home from there.' He glanced at her, smiling a little. 'You're not in a hurry to get back, are you? I thought we might have dinner at Oakham—there is a good hotel there and it is only a mile or two out of our way.' When she didn't answer at once, he added, 'I shall be glad of a rest by then.'

A remark calculated to make her feel instantly mean and thoughtless. 'Oh, of course you must rest. Isn't it a long way from York?'

'Not too far, we'll stop for a cup of tea somewhere.'

'Have you been this way before? I mean, you know

just where to go, don't you?'

'I have visited the general three or four times during the last year to so—he was a patient of mine when they lived for most of the year in London. Besides, I travel around quite a lot, you know.' He was looking straight ahead. 'I shall be going over to Holland shortly.'

'Not for always?' She was unaware of the dismay in her voice.

'No.' He sounded so cool suddenly; she was being nosy and, what was more, almost on the verge of letting him see that she would mind if he went away.

She said in a high voice, wooden with her efforts to sound casual, 'This is a very comfortable car for travelling . . .'

He agreed. 'So Mrs Pratt tells me.' His voice was silky and she sought wildly for a neutral topic of conversation before he dealt her a polite snub.

'Such a pity it looks like rain,' she began chattily.

He agreed for the second time and added, 'Rather worse than that, I believe; I was told before we left that there is very bad weather coming in from the north-east.'

'Oh, but won't we be going south? Away from it?'

'Hopefully. Do you have a raincoat with you?'

'Yes.'

He laughed a little. 'Of course you have—I can't imagine you being caught unawares about anything or anyone, Louise.'

Rather wide of the mark, she thought wryly, and make a matter-of-fact observation about the scenery.

Kelso looked interesting but he didn't pause, driving on to Jedburgh where he stopped at a pretty little café for coffee. It was beginning to rain as they got out of the car and the wind was gathering strength, but the weather, as far as Louise was concerned, didn't matter; she was with Aldo and she didn't intend to think about the future or anything else until she was back home and he wasn't there any more. Back in the car, he picked up the phone. 'I told Zoë I would ring her up when we stopped for coffee.' He was dialling the number and didn't look at her, and a moment later she heard him say, 'Zoë? We're at Jedburgh. I hope we will be back around about nine o'clock this evening. We shall have had a meal, so don't bother with any cooking.' He listened for a few moments, smiling, then, 'If you are still out of bed . . . But I shall see you when I pick you up tomorrow. Goodbye, my dear—have a word with Louise.'

'I'm so glad you're on the phone,' said Zoë in her ear. 'I've got this joint of lamb and I can't find your cookery book—how long do I roast it for?'

'Twenty minutes to the pound and twenty minutes over—get the oven hot first. Are you managing?'

'Rather; Miss Wills is a trump. She's just going off home in a minute or two; she says she will pop in to see you tomorrow.'

'Oh, good, dear. See you when we get back this evening.'

She handed the telephone back to Aldo, who said with some amusement, 'Having trouble with the roast? And I gather Miss Wills has endeared herself to the three of them. Most convenient,' he added thoughtfully.

She pondered that, not quite sure what he meant, and concluded that it meant nothing; she assured him that she was comfortable and they set off once more.

They were in the Cheviot Hills now and the country became dramatic, the lowering sky making it even more so. For a little while they drove through Redesdale Forest, which shut out the worsening weather, but presently they left the forest behind, in England again. With Ellishaw behind them the road ran ahead of them, lonely and bleak, and once they had gone through Ridsdale there were no villages. It was blowing a gale now and the rain had turned into a steady downpour, so Aldo slowed his speed. There was almost no traffic, the road was a good one and he drove with no sign of worry. At this rate, thought Louise, we shall never be home on time, but a delay of an hour or so wouldn't matter too much.

They spoke little, but she sensed a pleasant feeling of ease between them, like old friends who had no need to speak. A pity it couldn't be like this always, she thought wistfully; if she couldn't have his love she would settle for his friendship. As it was now, she still was not certain if he liked her all that much. As a nurse, yes, but as a woman? She didn't know.

They reached Corbridge and crossed the River Tyne and sped on, bypassing Darlington, taking the main road to Scotch Corner and joining the A1. It was plain sailing now, thought Louise; the road ran due south, and although there was more traffic Aldo was doing a steady seventy miles an hour, despite the appalling weather.

She glanced out of the window and saw the ominous blackness of the skyline and felt the wind gusting about the car. 'Nervous?' asked the doctor.

'Not in the least,' she told him, and meant it. 'This must be a freak storm. Perhaps it won't last.'

He grunted a reply, giving an elderly car a wide berth as he passed it. She watched his hands on the wheel; the car was holding the road well, but he was needing all his skill to drive. All the same, they made good time even though he took no risks, stopping for ten minutes or so in a small village south of Doncaster for a quick cup of tea and a sandwich in a convenient café, before driving on towards Newark. There was a good deal of water on the road by now, and here and there some flooding, and the rain was unceasing. It was unnaturally dark, so that the car's headlights reflected the rain and the doctor was forced to slow his pace. It wasn't all that far to go now; the road bypassed Newark and twenty minutes later Grantham, and within half an hour Aldo had turned off the road to take a country road to Oakham.

There was even more water on this road, and the fields on either side were waterlogged, but the hotel, standing on high ground sloping down to Rutland Water, was reasonably dry. It was still early evening, but already dark, and there were lights shining from most of the downstairs windows. Aldo stopped the car before the door and turned to look at Louise. 'I suppose if I had been sensible I would have driven straight back home because of this appalling weather, but something tells me that would have been a tame ending, wouldn't it? The least I can offer you is a good dinner after your calm acceptance of a wretched journey.'

She said in a small voice, 'I didn't find it wretched; I enjoyed it.'

'So did I.' He bent his head and kissed her swiftly and got out of the car. She was still getting over it when he opened her door and said with impassive good humour, 'Run for the door before you get soaked.' He draped her raincoat around her shoulders and she did as she was told; it was too wet and windy to argue.

The hotel was a splendid Victorian mansion, and delightful. She was led away to the powder room where she strove to repair the wear and tear of their journey. She was successful; indeed, save for a few damp patches where the raincoat hadn't quite covered her, she looked just as she always did: nicely made-up, her hair smoothly waved and combed . . . All the same, she frowned critically at her reflection before she went to join Aldo.

He took her to the bar and guided her to a small table well away from the counter. 'Sherry?' he asked her, and, when she said, 'Please,' nodded to the hovering waiter. 'And the menu, please.'

The menu cards came with the drinks and she was glad of that for Aldo was looking at her in a thoughtful way, half smiling, and she found it disconcerting. She buried her pretty nose in the menu and only glanced up when he suggested that they should have an asparagus mousse with chicken livers and truffles. 'And perhaps you like chicken? The mousseline of chicken with champagne sauce sounds good . . .'

It sounded mouth-watering. She agreed and added simply, 'I'm hungry.' And she blushed rosily. 'What I mean is, I wasn't a bit hungry at lunch time. The sandwiches were really very nice . . .'

He regarded her gravely, although there was a really pronounced twinkle in his eyes. 'Louise, why are you always so careful not to annoy me? Am I such an ogre?

Is that how you thought of me at St Nicholas's when I was called in and disrupted your nights?'

'No, never, and—and I'm not careful, only I said something that made me sound ungrateful. Sometimes,' she told him ingenuously, 'I say things that don't come out just as I mean them to.'

'I must remember that.' He handed the menus back to the waiter and sat back comfortably in his chair. 'How pleasant to sit and chat for a while.' His voice was bland. 'We had so little chance to talk at the general's house, and driving conditions made conversation rather spasmodic.'

Louise sipped her sherry. 'What do you want to talk about?'

'You.'

'Me? Whatever for?'

'I know so little about you. Until recently you were firmly entrenched behind your uniform and very correct manner, and when I got to know you rather better, you retreated behind a cool façade heavily larded with domesticity. Very hard to penetrate. I must admit that just once or twice you forgot who I was and talked to me as though I were a friend.' He said deliberately, 'Don't you like me, Louise?'

'Yes, oh, yes—of course I do, but just like you, until recently I saw you as a senior consultant whom I only met occasionally and knew nothing about.' She had spoken with commendable calm, pleased with her sensible answer.

'That is exactly what I had expected you to say. One day you shall give me the real answer.'

It seemed best to ignore that. She took another sip of sherry. 'Mike and Christine think you are super, and

Zoë talks about you all the time.'

It was an opening if he wanted to talk about her sister, but it seemed he didn't. 'And you, Louise—what do you think of me?'

She should have expected that. 'I don't know you well enough to know.'

He laughed then, not, she thought, at her, but at something else which he found amusing. She put down her empty glass. 'This is a very pleasant hotel . . .'

'One of the best in the country.' He made no effort to enlarge upon that, so she was left to seek another topic of conversation from a head empty of all ideas. It was fortunate that they were invited to go into the restaurant, another splendid room which provided a talking point for several minutes.

The food was delicious and she was hungry, but annoyance grew as the meal progressed, for Aldo was leaving her to do the talking; answering her readily but making no effort to introduce any ideas of his own. Perhaps he was bored? She cast a quick look at him across the table and found his eyes fixed on her with a curious intentness, so much so that she put up a hand to her hair to make sure that it hadn't come loose from its french pleat.

He said gently, 'There's nothing wrong. I like it when you tie your hair back.'

She said weakly, 'Oh, do you? But that is only when I'm at home.' She grew pink. 'I have to put it up when I'm in uniform or—or going out.' She heard herself babbling and she was quite unable to stop. 'Christine's got lovely hair, but Zoë has naturally waving hair and it's as gold as guineas.'

'Yes. I had noticed.' His voice was dry. He took the menu he was offered. 'What would you like for a sweet?'

She bent her head over her own menu. 'Strawberry ice in a pastry case—that sounds heavenly. I'd like that, please.'

He ordered it, and cheese for himself, and glanced at his watch.

'Should we be going? Have we been here too long?'

He shook his head. 'No, I was wondering if it mattered very much if we didn't get back as early as I said we would. Half an hour over coffee in the drawing-room here would be nice.'

She said at once, 'Well, could you not telephone Zoë and let her know?' She added, 'It's delightful here, isn't it? I wonder if it's still raining?'

The ice came and she ate it with unselfconscious pleasure, and presently they went to the drawing-room and sat side by side on a comfortable sofa before the fire with the coffee-table beside them. They had been among the earliest diners and, beyond a handful of people getting up a game of bridge at the other end of the large room, there was no one else there.

Perhaps it was her surroundings or the splendid meal she had just had, but Louise was no longer annoyed. Aldo sat beside her, not saying much, but somehow there didn't seem any need to talk. Presently he said quietly, 'I think we should go; there's an hour and a half more to drive.'

She said, 'Is that all?' before she could stop herself and followed that by a falsely bright, 'It will be nice to be home again.'

'You haven't enjoyed the trip?'

'I've loved every minute of it.' She checked herself just in time from letting her tongue run away with her. 'Scotland is beautiful,' she finished tamely.

He put down his coffee-cup. 'Yes, we must go again some time.' A remark which left her wondering what on earth he meant.

It was dark by now and still raining, but they made good time until they reached the point on the A1 where Aldo turned off to take the cross-country road which would bring them to Much Hadham. There was little traffic by now and Louise, lulled by the incessant rain, was half asleep when she heard the doctor utter an outlandish word she didn't understand—Dutch, she thought—and sat up, wide awake.

The road ahead of them was awash, and as he slowed the car the lights picked out chaos. The road turned in a gentle bend and on the bend there had been a cottage, built sideways on to the road, its walls protruding to its edge. At least, they *had* protruded; now they lay in a heap of rubble in the road, entangled with two twisted wrecks of cars.

The doctor reached behind him and picked up his bag, opened his door and shrugged into his car coat. 'Phone the police, Louise, and the ambulance and fire brigade, and then stay here.'

Nothing happened when she dialled. She wasted minutes trying again and again, and finally put the receiver back, struggled into her raincoat and got out of the car. Ahead of her she could see the wreckage quite clearly in the car's lights, and someone was there with a torch. Aldo, she supposed. She went back to the car and opened the glove compartment and found what she had hoped for, another torch, and with this in her hand she waded to where she had seen his light. Now she was near enough she could hear cries and voices calling and a baby crying, but she didn't stop until she fetched up very wet and breathless beside Aldo.

'The phone's dead,' she told him, ignoring his angry voice telling her to go back. 'And I'm not going back. There is a baby crying; I'm going to find it—it's in the house.'

A hand clamped her to a standstill. 'You will not go into the house.' The doctor sounded furiously angry in a cold and quite frightening way. 'It's liable to collapse at any moment.' He pushed his powerful torch into her hand and took hers. 'There is a woman here, not too badly hurt; get her out of the way—the other side of the road—there's a bank there above the water.'

She said urgently, 'Aldo, take care . . .' He had gone. The woman was one of the lucky ones, dazed and bruised and half hysterical, but easy to free from the remnants of the back of the car. Louise heaved her clear, helped her to the bank, bade her stay there and went back to see who else she could free. The water seemed to be rising; it would be the small river alongside the road, one of several which riddled the country roads around Stevenage and the surrounding villages. Louise knew where she was; the cottage was a lone dwelling between the turnings to two villages. They must have passed the lane to Westmill, lying a little way off the road. In this weather and on such a dark night she doubted if anyone would have heard the crash above the wind and the rain. She set the torch down on a bit of wreckage and began to ease out an elderly woman through a broken door.

'Can you move everything?' she asked. 'Will you try

your legs? I think your arms are all right.'

The woman nodded and Louise bent to her task once more, to be interrupted by the doctor. He had a blanketed bundle under one arm, while the other supported a young woman. 'Get them to the bank,' he told Louise, and thrust the baby at her. 'Her husband is still inside. He has a fractured leg. We must get him out.'

'Give me two ticks,' said Louise.

The little house was still intact on the side furthest from the road, but with each gust of wind a few more tiles came tumbling down, and the groans and creaks of the woodwork became more ominous. The man had been in the kitchen, which was fortunate; she found broom handles and tea towels with which to tie amateur splints and, while Aldo dealt with them, collected an armful of nappies to serve as bandages. The man was young, thin and on the small side; the doctor heaved him up and waded back across the road and laid his burden down by the others. They were wet to the skin, but at least they were comparatively safe.

Aldo bent over the elderly woman. 'How many in your car?' he asked her gently, and then straightened up. 'The driver—we'd better get at him next. There are two young boys—teenagers—in the other car. One is unconscious, the other is cut about the face.'

They toiled together to free the driver, unconscious too, which made it easier to move him. They got him clear at last and on to the bank and roughly bandaged where he had cut his head, and as they made their way through the flood Louise clutched Aldo's arm, shouting above the wind.

'Look, I know where we are. It's only ten minutes'

walk to a village close by—there'll be a telephone there. I'll try from there, if not I'll get someone to go back to Buntingford. There's a police house there . . .'

'It's not safe for you to go.' For a moment he put a great arm around her. 'But I'll have to let you do it, there's not any other way.'

He pulled her close, almost breaking her ribs, and then let her go. 'Be careful!' He turned away to help the two boys, and she began her difficult scramble back to the turning. The water wasn't so high here, and she could get along faster, and presently she saw a few lights ahead of her. The village was small and she banged on the first door she stumbled against.

No one came; she banged again and shouted, and this time the door did open. The man looked at her standing there, streaming water and muddy.

'What's up, love?' he asked, and then, over his shoulder, 'Mother . . .'

His wife peered over his shoulder, and Louise said urgently, 'A telephone—is there one here? There's been a bad accident up on the main road—the cottage and two cars, and the road is flooded.'

The man was quick to understand. 'The telephone's across the road, but I doubt if it's working—I'll go and see . . .'

The woman urged Louise inside and she stood dripping all over the floor of the little hall, almost dancing with impatience. He was back very quickly. 'The line is dead.' He was getting into boots and winding a long scarf over his jacket. 'I'll walk into Buntingford, there's a constable there. You stay here, miss, and dry off.'

'Bless you for going, but I can't. I'm travelling with

a doctor; he's there at the scene giving first aid—I'm a nurse, so I can give him some help.'

She was glad of the man's company along the lane, and at the main road they parted without loss of time, he to make his way to Buntingford, she back to the shambles by the cottage.

The doctor was bending over one of the young boys, examining his head. He looked up briefly. 'OK?' and when she nodded, out of breath, 'Good. This boy is badly concussed; try and keep him still.' He got to his feet and started to make his way towards the house.

'Where are you going?' Louise raised her voice in an urgent shout, afraid to be left alone.

'Round the back of the house. I'll be back.' He sounded so calm that she felt ashamed of her anxious shout. Once he had disappeared into the darkness on the other side of the road she got down on her knees in the water lapping the bank and did her best to hold down the boy. She was a strong girl and well used to dealing with recalcitrant patients, but he was a hefty youth and she had her work cut out, and while she struggled with him, trying to keep him still, she worried about the other figures lying or sitting around her; they all needed attention, some more than others; she wished that Aldo would come back.

When he did, a few moments later, he was carrying a shopping bag, and by the car's headlights she could make out a cat inside; a greatly frightened, bad-tempered cat, venting its fear on the night air, adding to the groans and voices around her. Beside him was a dog, splashing along uttering short, enquiring barks. The man from the cottage gave a whistle and the dog scrambled to him, and the doctor handed the bag to the man's wife.

The doctor paused for a moment, an enormous figure in the gloom, and Louise knew why; there was a faint smell of burning, hot and rubbery; she hoped that no one else had noticed it. The bank they were on was several yards from the wreckage, but if there was a fire, it would be fierce, despite the rain. Aldo loomed beside her.

'I think we should try and move everyone along the bank. You take the woman and baby first, get to the corner if you can manage it, and then come back here.'

She did as he had asked her without speaking, and waded back in time to see a small flame flickering somewhere in the tangle of cars. Perhaps the water would put it out, she hoped, and, obedient to Aldo's word, hauled the two women in turn back to where she had put the mother and baby.

The doctor had carried the man with the broken leg and set him down beside his wife with the dog and the cat. He went back at once and returned with the elderly man, still unconscious, then turned to go again. The little flame had spread; Louise took one look and splashed after him. 'I can help one of the boys, if you can carry the other.'

They were well clear when the little flame found the petrol tank of one of the cars; all the same, Louise let out a yell of pure fright. The doctor, arranging his burden tidily on the wet grass, said with calm, 'Now someone somewhere will see us.'

She hadn't thought of that. It's an ill wind . . . she told herself, trying to stop shaking, not sure if it was from fright or cold; a bit of both, she supposed.

They had been seen; the man from the village had

reached the police house, sensibly borrowed a motorbike since the telephone was out of order and made his way to Stevenage, while the constable got into his car and battled his way towards the fire, now glowing brightly. He was a stolid man of good sense; he took over the care of the restless boy and left Louise free to wrap the blankets he had brought with him round the others.

Presently help arrived, the fire was put out, the ambulance loaded their patients and drove away, and the police took names and addresses.

The doctor urged Louise back into the car, then went away to talk to one of the police and then to the man who had come to their help. He came back with him soon and ushered him into the back of the car.

'We will have to go to the hospital,' he told Louise briefly, 'and on the way I'll drop off Mr Coombes.' He added quietly, 'We cannot thank you enough for your help, you may have saved several lives.'

'Glad to help,' said the man bashfully.

The doctor got out of his car at the cottage and went inside with him after Louise had added her thanks. She could see the doctor talking to the man's wife, then they all shook hands and he got into the car beside her again.

He started the engine and then put a hand on her knee. 'You're tired. I'll be as quick as I can. Will Zoë be worried?'

'I don't think so—she knows what the weather is like and that it would slow you down.'

'When you get home, have a hot drink and a hot bath and go straight to bed; stay there tomorrow if you don't feel good.'

She said quickly, 'I shall be quite all right after a night's sleep. I'm only wet.' She glanced at his dim shape. 'So are you.'

They were driving back the way they had come to go to Stevenage. She would be able to telephone Zoë from the hospital; there was bound to be a wait there while Aldo saw whoever was on duty in the casualty department.

'The dog and cat,' she said suddenly.

'The young woman from the house has a sister in Stevenage. I told the ambulanceman to drive her there first and park her and the baby and the animals. The address is close to the hospital and it will only take a few minutes.'

'You think of everything,' muttered Louise, 'and you always know just what to do.'

'Not always,' said the doctor softly.

As he got out of the car at the hospital he said, 'I'll telephone Zoë.' He tucked the rug he had wrapped her in more tightly round her shoulders. 'I'll not be long.'

He wasn't, and very shortly afterwards he was helping her out of the car in front of Ivy Cottage. 'Go in,' he told her. 'I'll bring your bag.'

Zoë was still up, wrapped in a dressing-gown, looking so pretty, with huge sleepy eyes and her hair a mass of golden curls. She flung her arms around Louise.

'Darling, you're soaked. I've got tea made and the bath's ready for you, just as Aldo said.' She flung an arm round him then and kissed him.

Louise's heart lurched painfully at the sight, but all

she said was, 'You'll have some tea, Aldo?'

'No, thanks all the same. I'll get home. Zoë, give me a ring in the morning if Louise doesn't feel like getting up.' He grinned tiredly. 'Thank you, Louise—not quite the ending I had hoped for, but the best-laid plans, etc . . . Goodnight!'

He got back into the damp car and drove away, and Louise drank her tea, then, escorted by Zoë, went upstairs, took off her wet clothes and lay in a very hot bath while she recounted her adventures.

Zoë was a good listener; she hardly interrupted at all and at the end exclaimed, 'What a blessing Aldo was with you; he always knows what to do, doesn't he? Don't you think he's marvellous?' She peered at Louise through the steam.

'Oh, yes, he's very dependable.' Louise made her voice casually interested. 'You like him, don't you, Zoë?'

'I think he's super. I've put a hot-water bottle in your bed, and you'd better get out of the bath before the water gets cold.'

There was a great deal to think about once she was in bed, and Zoë, too, but Louise went to sleep immediately.

She awoke at her usual time, and beyond a bruise or two on her legs where she had stumbled during her walk to the village she felt just as usual. She got up, called the others and started breakfast for them all. Christine and Mike both came down to the kitchen in their nightclothes, annoyed that no one had seen fit to wake them up to join in the excitement.

'Well, we weren't all that excited,' observed Louise sensibly. 'Look, go and dress, my dears. I'm going to have breakfast, otherwise Aldo will go without me. Zoë will be down in a minute.'

She fed Dusty and went to telephone Aldo, feeling the now familiar little thrill at the sound of his voice.

'You're sure you feel fit for a day's work?' he wanted to know, and then, 'Very well, I will be outside in half an hour.'

Beyond a few casual remarks about their previous evening he had little to say. He had a round at the hospital as well as several private patients to see; it was going to be a busy day, thought Louise, but didn't say so. He looked tired, although he was as immaculate as he always was. He had probably been up for hours, telephoning Stevenage, reading his mail and working at his desk; she had too much sense to ask.

The day was as busy as she had expected it to be. The last private patient didn't go until almost five o'clock, and her heart sank when Aldo came into the examination room where she was tidying up and told her that he was going back to St Nicholas's, but she said, 'Very well, Doctor, I'll lock up as I go, shall I? Will it be all right if I let the porter have the keys, or shall I leave them at your house?'

'Neither. You're almost ready, aren't you? I'll wait for you and take the keys. I'm so sorry I can't take you home, but I will drop you off at the nearest bus stop.'

He stood leaning against the door watching her fold blankets and put out fresh towels and cover her little trolley. She did it all speedily but with great neatness, and presently closed the last drawer and cupboard.

'I'll get my things.'

He glanced at his watch. 'You're tired—so am I—and there's not time to talk. Perhaps tomorrow. I shall want

you to come with me to Holland next week, Louise.'
And, when she stood stock still, gaping at him, 'I must
ask you to be quick . . .'

She got her outdoor things and without a word went
out to the car with him and got into it. The bus which
would start her on her way home stopped a couple of
streets away; he pulled up to the kerb and she opened
her door, ready to get out quickly. His kiss was just a
little quicker and he said something softly, in his own
language, she presumed, for she didn't understand a
word. She jumped out without a backward glance and
joined the bus queue, and when she did turn her head
the car was no longer there.

CHAPTER EIGHT

IF AFTER a wakeful night Louise had hoped to have an explanation from Aldo, she was doomed to disappointment. Beyond a cheerful good morning and the lowering observation that they had a busy day ahead of them, he had nothing much to say, and when they reached his rooms he just dropped her off with a quick nod and drove himelf off to St Nicholas's. He didn't come back before his first patient was due to arrive and Louise, with everything ready and waiting and nothing much to do but answer Miss Squires's eager questions about the road accident, was glad to see him; now she could plunge into the day's routine and bury her troublesome thoughts.

Only they would not be buried. How could they be with him sitting behind his desk, calm and remote, listening to his patients' complaints, examining them, reassuring them, telling them what he intended to do for them, holding out a hand for forms or whatever, barely glancing at her when he asked her to undress the patient, fetch notes, or take a temperature?

Outwardly her usual serene self, she pondered his announcement—not even a request—that she was to go to Holland with him. It was, to say the least of it, infuriating not to know why and where. While she divested an elderly lady of her outer garments, she made a mental note to refuse to go . . .

The patient was difficult, worried that her hair would be disarranged and unwilling to remove the several gold chains around her neck. Louise made soothing noises, assured that lady that not a hair was out of place and settled her on the couch ready for Aldo to examine. The patient was ill, but obstinately refusing to believe it; Louise listened to Aldo gently charming her into accepting the fact and agreeing to go into hospital for treatment. He did it very well, she considered; his bedside manner was faultless; moreover, it was genuine.

The next patient was a bluff, elderly man whose symptoms had to be wormed from him gradually. He disliked discussing illness, and informed the doctor that if it hadn't been for his wife persuading him he would never have come in the first place. The doctor listened with a patient ear, sitting back in his chair as though he had all day empty in front of him, instead of a string of patients waiting their turn.

The last one for the morning went just before one o'clock, and Miss Squires prepared to go to her lunch. 'You have got your sandwiches, dear?' she wanted to know. 'We shall be busy again this afternoon, so do take it easy for an hour. There's plenty of tea in the cupboard if you don't want coffee.' She took herself off and Louise went back to tidy the examination room ready for the afternoon. The doctor was still in his consulting room with the door shut, but he would go out presently to wherever he went at lunch time. She finished what she was doing and went to the tiny kitchenette to put on the kettle.

'No, you won't need that,' said Aldo from the doorway. 'I'm going across to the pub; I'd like you to come with me. I can explain about the trip to Holland while we eat.'

She still had her hand on the kettle. 'I would rather not go to Holland, if you don't mind.'

'I do mind. You have a reason?'

'Well . . .' She couldn't go on. To invent a reason on the spur of the moment was beyond her; besides, she was a poor liar.

'Well, Louise?' And, when she still said nothing. 'I hate to remind you, but you are in my employ.'

Slow colour flooded her face; she stood still, still holding the kettle, staring at him. He stared back, his face expressionless.

'Unless your reason is one of life and death, my dear, you will come with me.' There was no hint of annoyance in his level voice.

He was quite right, of course. She got her outdoor things and accompanied him down the street, to turn down a narrow lane lined with small shops. The pub was on the corner and when they went in it was obvious that he was known there, for the bartender looked up with a cheerful, 'Morning, sir—the usual?'

'Morning, Tom. Yes, please, and perhaps the lady might have the menu?'

She was ushered to a small table in the end booth, and Aldo sat down opposite her. 'Coffee?' he said quietly while she studied the card.

'Yes, and sandwiches please. Brown bread, prawns and salad.'

Tom went away and Aldo said easily, 'I come here frequently. If I stay at St Nicholas's we only talk shop. It's nice to get away.'

The coffee came and then the sandwiches and the

doctor's beer. The pub was almost full, but there was no one in the next booth. Louise poured her coffee from a generous pot on the table and waited for Aldo to speak.

'We go to Utrecht next Tuesday and we shall be there for four, perhaps five days. I've asked Miss Squires to fit in as many patients before then as can be managed—I'm afraid you may be working late for the rest of the week. My registrar will take over at the hospitals until we are back.'

Louise bit into a sandwich. 'Where . . . That is, is it a hospital you're going to?' She took another bite. 'In Utrecht?'

'I've some examining to do there, but I have also been asked to give a second opinion on two patients of a colleague of mine—an old friend.'

'Do I stay at the hospital?'

'No. This colleague, Litrik van Rijgen, lives with his wife near Ziest—that is a town close to Utrecht; it is two of his patients whom I am to examine. You shall stay with them. His wife is English—Francesca—a nurse before she married. They have a baby son.'

'I have no passport.'

'Go to the post office and get a visitor's passport—they'll do it there and then. In fact, we'll get the forms on our way back to the rooms.'

Louise poured a second cup of coffee and watched the last of the sandwiches being eaten. There was no use in making a fuss, Aldo had made up his mind that she was to go with him to Holland, and nothing she could say would make any difference; indeed, he might be wondering why she was so reluctant; after all, it would make a nice change any girl would jump at. Not

that she wasn't only too willing to jump at it, but
prudence reminded her that seeing too much of him was
asking for trouble. On the other hand, she reflected, it
might be an opportunity to find out just how interested
he was in Zoë and encourage him . . .

She said serenely, 'Very well, I'm quite ready when
you are, Doctor.'

'Aldo.' He got up and went to the bar and paid, and
they walked the short distance to the post office in the
busy main road at the end of the lane. Having collected
the passport forms, they walked back to his rooms. They
got there with five minutes to spare, to find Miss Squires
agitated at their absence. 'I've phoned the patients you
wanted to transfer to this week, Doctor,' she started as
soon as they were indoors. 'Only two of them are unable
to change their appointments, Lady Henny and Mr
Evans. They agreed to come the following week, same
day, same time.'

The doctor paused on his way to his consulting room.
'Splendid, Miss Squires. I knew I could depend on you.
While we are away there is no need for you to come in
every day. Switch on the answering machine and—let
me see, we go on Tuesday and probably return on
Saturday evening—could you pop in on Thursday and
deal with anything urgent? I will leave my telephone
number.'

He shut the door behind him and Louise tore out of
her coat and scarf, perched her cap just so on her head
and joined Miss Squires until such time as the first
patient arrived.

The rest of the week went by quickly; Aldo seemed
indefatigable and apparently expected Miss Squires and
Louise to be the same, but since he put Miss Squires into

a taxi on the two evenings when they were delayed until almost seven o'clock, and drove Louise to and from his rooms each day, to complain would have been silly; besides, he wouldn't have listened anyway.

Louise had told Zoë about the trip to Holland with some trepidation, adding, 'You don't mind me going, Zoë? I am working for Aldo and he's in the habit of taking a nurse with him when he goes to see those patients of his.' She looked at her sister doubtfully. 'You're sure you'll be able to manage? Miss Wills might come again, just once more. I should think Aldo's nurse will be back soon, and I will get a job where I can be home normally.'

She could detect no disquiet in Zoë's manner, and when she told Mike and Christine they were enchanted. 'Oh, good—will you bring back something really Dutch? They're supposed to make gorgeous chocolates. Will you get a chance to explore?'

Louise explained about the friend who was going to put her up.

'And Aldo, where will he go?'

'I've no idea.' For once Louise sounded slightly peevish, and her sisters and brother exchanged glances.

It was the next morning, while Louise was getting coffee for the three of them, that Miss Squires, going into the consulting room with some notes, left the door open and Louise overheard Aldo telephoning.

'I think we had better wait until we are back again before we say anything, Zoë. You haven't talked about it at all?' There was a short pause, then, 'You need not feel guilty, my dear . . .' Miss Squires, with more notes, went in again and this time shut the door.

Louise stood watching the kettle boil its head off and

did nothing about it. She admonished herself; hadn't she known all this time that Aldo and Zoë . . .? But now her vague guesses and surmises had been made concrete, and there was no loophole for hope to creep in.

The trip to Holland suddenly became a nightmare, instead of the exciting few days she had been looking forward to, at least in part. Not that she had expected Aldo to be anything but his rather remote self, friendly and kind and thoughtful and quite impersonal, but just being with him would have made her happy.

She turned off the gas at last and made the coffee, just as Miss Squires came bustling along to see what had kept her so long. 'There's that Mrs Pettigrew due in ten minutes, and you know how the doctor hates to drink his coffee in a hurry,' she said reproachfully. 'I'll take it in as I go.'

Normally no patients came on a Saturday morning, but since the doctor was to be away, three of them had elected to come for a consultation then. 'None of them will take long,' Aldo told Louise as they drove to London on Saturday, 'but they are patients I like to see frequently—all heart cases. I shall go straight to St Nicholas's afterwards, and I'm afraid I'm not sure how long I shall be. Can you get yourself back home?'

'Easily. Is Miss Squires coming in as well?'

'Yes. Louise, when you get back to Ivy Cottage, will you ask Zoë to come over this evening? I've a book for her.'

Louise was looking out of the window, and her voice was quite steady as she told him that of course she would tell her.

Zoë looked mischievous when Louise passed the message on, and directly after supper she left the house with the remark that she wouldn't be long. The two younger ones were in bed and Louise was setting the table ready for breakfast before she returned. True, she had a book under her arm, but she looked very pleased with herself. Louise debated with herself as to whether it would be a good idea to tell her sister that she knew all about it and there was no need to be so secretive about it. On the other hand, Zoë must have some very good reason for not saying anything.

She thought that she knew the reason by the time they went up to bed, for over a cup of tea Zoë had asked, 'Do you ever feel that you are missing something, Louise? I mean, you have had years of looking after us and making ends meet and never going out or having boy-friends. We've been selfish, I dare say, letting you cope with everything—me, especially——And supposing I was to get married and leave you to look after Mike and Christine when it ought to be the other way round—you getting married and me taking over the household?'

Louise poured more tea with a steady hand and in a voice just as steady said, 'Zoë, darling, I'm happy and content as I am, and I would be so very pleased if you married someone who would take care of you and love you. And I don't have to cope any more, do I? Not now we have Ivy Cottage.'

'When Aldo's nurse comes back again you'll be without a job once more.'

'Oh, pooh to that. There are plenty of jobs around; they seem to drop into my lap.'

'Don't you want to get married?' persisted Zoë.

Louise said lightly, 'Me? Darling, perhaps one day, when I have time.' She had even managed an amused laugh.

Thankfully she was busy on Sunday: church in the morning and a small case to pack after lunch, watched minutely by her sisters telling her what to take with her. Finally she said, half laughing, 'Look, dears, I'm only going for four or five days and it's not a holiday, you know, I'm going to work . . .'

'Not all the time, you can't, only if Aldo is working too,' observed Christine. 'And if you're staying with these friends of his you can't sit down to dinner in your overall. Wear the blue you wore to Scotland, pack your green dress, and take the grey crêpe just in case.'

'But I shall never wear it.'

'You can squash it up in a corner, and it'll be there if you want it.'

Miss Wills had to be visited, and displayed no reluctance to return at such short notice and certainly no surprise, a fact which escaped Louise's notice, since her head was full of the various instructions she wanted to give to Zoë. Of Aldo there was no sign, although she hadn't really expected to see him; it was Zoë who told her while they sat at tea that he had gone to spend the day with old friends—somewhere in Essex, she thought, adding that it was a pity because there was something she wanted to see him about. She glanced at Louise as she said it, but Louise had taught herself to be on her guard against such remarks; she observed sensibly that Zoë would be able to see him on Monday. 'For we don't go until Tuesday afternoon; Aldo has a round at St Nicholas's in the morning and some private patients he particularly wants to see before he goes.'

The doctor occupied the drive to his rooms on Monday morning with details of the two patients he was to see in Holland. Louise listened carefully, for the simple reason that he expected her to, and to remember what he had said, too. He was away all the morning, and in the afternoon she was kept more than busy, for the patients who had appointments, ill though they were, were pernickety. She bore with them, for that was part of her job, and as for Aldo, he exhibited the patience of Job and unfailing good humour. He was silent on their journey back to Much Hadham, and she made no attempt to talk. Something was on his mind; she could see that with eyes sharpened by love. Possibly it was one of his patients.

She got into the blue outfit the next morning and felt a rising excitement at the prospect of going to Holland, but she damped it down with the reflection that she would most likely see little of Aldo outside her nursing duties; she must contrive to keep out of his way . . .

She was seen off in a flurry of hugs and kisses and requests to bring back something Dutch, never mind what, just as long as it was the real thing. Louise, conscious of Aldo sitting patiently waiting for her, hugged them all once more, gave Dusty a final pat and got into the car.

'I wonder,' observed the doctor pensively, 'if any man will be able to prise you from your family?'

She bit back the words 'you could' just in time, and answered in a matter-of-fact voice, 'Well, the question doesn't arise, does it?'

He didn't answer but presently said, 'I've got seats on an early afternoon flight from Heathrow; we shall have to leave just after one o'clock, so get some lunch before that if you can.'

'Oh, yes, well . . . I thought we were going by ferry?'

'I changed my mind. I'll leave the car at the airport; there will be a car for us at Schiphol.'

As it turned out there was no time for lunch; the

patient who was to have arrived at eleven o'clock telephoned to say that he would not be coming until midday, and since he had several good reasons for this there was nothing to be done about it. Louise, having put everything in apple pie order, had coffee with Miss Squires and when the doctor returned from the hospital, gave him a cup, too, and left him to work in his consulting room until the patient arrived. He was a well-known man in public life and, besides being ill, possessed a bad temper and a stubborn wish to have everything done to his way of thinking. It took the doctor's calm bedside manner and Louise's gentle wheedling to get him to see things their way, and when finally he had gone there was barely time to get into the car and drive to Heathrow.

The flight was too short for Louise, taken as it was in the comfort of first class with coffee and sandwiches, and Aldo beside her—immersed in papers it was true, but still, there.

Beyond making sure that she had all that she wanted and was comfortable, he had little to say, and at Schiphol he went briskly through Customs and out to the reception hall with a porter carrying their bags, to be met by a short, stout man dressed very neatly in dark blue, with a round, jovial face and a fringe of hair round a bald head.

'Pieter,' said the doctor briefly to Louise, and said something to the man in Dutch. Pieter gave her a little bow and shook hands, and led the way out of the hall, across the narrow street to where cars were parked.

He stopped by a dark grey Rolls-Royce and opened the door, and Aldo said, 'Get in, Louise. We have half an hour's drive to Utrecht.'

He ushered her into the back, to get behind the wheel himself while Pieter got in the front beside him. Louise sat contemplating Aldo's vast back, trying to decide whether the car had been hired or whether it belonged to this friend of his; it wouldn't be Aldo's, he had his own car in England. She gave up speculating presently and turned her attention to the scenery: motorway with everything going very fast and flat country on either side, but soon they were on another motorway to Utrecht and she could see lakes on either side of the road and then the outskirts of the city. Aldo kept straight on, skirting it before turning east towards Zeist. He slowed his speed now and turned into a country road, leaving Zeist behind them, too, going through pleasantly wooded country. They soon reached a small village, with tiny cottages seemingly dwarfed by a very large church which he passed before turning into an open gateway between pillars. In a moment he stopped before a flight of semi-circular steps leading to the front door of a solid, flat-faced house of some size.

'Is this it?' asked Louise.

'Yes.' Aldo got out and opened her door, and Pieter went to the boot and got the bags out as the door opened to allow a tall man with fair hair sprinkled with grey and a smallish woman with mousy hair and a plain face full of charm to hurry down the steps.

The doctor gave her a hug and kiss, shook hands with the man and turned to Louise. 'Fran, Litrik, this is Louise. Louise, they are among my oldest friends . . .'

They welcomed her with a warmth which dispelled the slight feelings of apprehension which had been creeping over her, and Francesca took her arm and led the way indoors. 'Come up to your room,' she invited, 'then we'll have tea. You must be dying for a cup.'

She ushered Louise through the hall and up the rather grand staircase, saying, 'You're in the bedroom I had when I first came here . . .' She broke off to exclaim, 'Hark at Thor and Muff!—they dote on Aldo—dogs, you know . . .'

She crossed a wide gallery and opened a door. 'I hope you'll be comfy, Louise. I was so awfully glad when Aldo said he would be bringing you. I'll leave you for five minutes, shall I?' She went to the door. 'You're just as pretty as he said you were.' She nodded her neat head, smiling, and went away.

The room was large and beautiful and there was a bathroom beyond as well as a balcony. Louise did her face and her hair and was ready when Francesca tapped on the door.

'Would you like to see our baby?' she wanted to know, and led the way along a short corridor to a room at the back of the house. It was light and airy, and there was a plump young woman with a kind face sitting by the window, and close by a very small baby in a cot.

'Benedict Litrik,' said his mother proudly, 'and this is Nanny, one of the pillars of the household.'

Nanny smiled widely and shook hands, and Louise went to bend over the cot. The son of the house was asleep; he looked, she thought, like his father in miniature. 'He's gorgeous,' she said, and she meant it. 'How old is he?'

'Two months. I bath him each evening while Nanny has her supper and half an hour's peace—if you like, you can come, too?'

'Oh, I'd love to.'

The two of them went down to join the men in the

drawing-room, and found them sitting in two great arm-chairs with the dogs between them: a mastiff and a small dog with a long, curly coat and obscure parentage.

The men got up as they went in, and Louise found herself beside her host, quite put at her ease by his gentle flow of small talk. Aldo had hardly spoken to her, but presently Francesca said, 'Why don't you take Louise round the garden, Aldo? It's too early to bath Benedict, and once you two get together there'll be no prising you apart.'

The garden was large and rambling, and as they crossed the lawn Louise remarked upon its beauty, her voice rather high and wooden because she was feeling shy and not quite certain if Aldo had wanted to join her. His manners were far too good for him to refuse his hostess's suggestion, but Louise wasn't sure if he had been all that keen.

They wandered around while she kept up a conversation of sorts until she said with a touch of peevishness, 'Well, shall we go back? I expect you are wishing to talk to your friend . . .'

For answer he took her arm and turned her round to face him. 'No, I have no desire to go indoors; walking here with you and listening to you talking is very restful, and if I don't talk it is because my thoughts are so pleasant that I would not wish to disturb them.'

She stood, his hands on her shoulders, looking up into his quiet face. She could think of nothing to say, but her heart was in her eyes, while thoughts raced and tumbled around inside her head, but at last it cleared sufficiently for her to say in a small voice, 'Zoë would love it here.'

'So she would.' He spoke lightly, but he sighed, too, and took his hands from her shoulders and began to stroll on once more. 'I must tell you about tomorrow. Litrik will meet us at his patient's house in Utrecht at half-past ten. She is an elderly lady, very nervous. She speaks and understands English, and I know you will do your best to keep her calm. You have already seen her case history, so you know more or less what to expect. She is autocratic and can sometimes be rude. I dare say we shall be there for a couple of hours. I shall go to Utrecht to the hospital with Litrik, but one of us will drive you back here first. The second patient has an appointment for Thursday afternoon; we'll talk about her later.'

They were retracing their steps now and a few minutes later Louise went off with Francesca to the nursery and, as for the rest of the evening, delightful though it was, she exchanged barely a dozen words with him.

She did not sleep very well, despite the comfort of her bed, and went down to breakfast with a pale face and shadows under her eyes. Francesca eyed her appreciatively.

'Heavens, but you are pretty,' she declared. 'I simply can't think why you haven't been snapped up long ago. I like the cap, don't you, Litrik?'

Her husband studied it carefully. 'Very much, very becoming. You looked quite enchanting in yours, darling.'

His wife beamed at him across the table. 'You do say the nicest things. Aldo, when you marry, remember to compliment your wife at the breakfast table, it starts the day off very nicely!'

Aldo passed his cup for more coffee. 'I'll bear it in mind, Fran.' He was smiling and she said at once, 'Oh, are you going to marry at last?'

'Oh, yes.'

Francesca opened her mouth to speak, then shut it again at her husband's look. 'I'm glad. Louise, have another of these rolls. Will you have time to say hello to Benedict before you go?'

'Ten o'clock at the door,' said Aldo.

It was actually five minutes to the hour when Louise crossed the hall to find Aldo waiting, talking to Tuggs, the van Rijgens' manservant.

Tuggs opened the door and Louise passed through and paused on the steps to wave to Francesca, who was hanging out of the nursery window. The Rolls-Royce was there again, and as she got in she remarked, 'Litrik doesn't mind you driving his car? Didn't he go off in a Daimler this morning? Two such super cars . . .'

'Er, yes . . . This one happens to be mine.'

She turned to stare at him. 'Yours? But you've got a car in England.'

He sounded almost apologetic. 'Well, yes. This one is kept at my home—my parents' home—and when I come over here Pieter drives it down for me.'

She digested this in silence, while questions bubbled on her tongue. She heard his gentle laugh. 'So many questions and no time to answer them all—not just yet, anyhow.'

They were on the outskirts of Utrecht. 'A pity there is so little time to show you the city. There's the Dom Tower ahead—four hundred and sixty-five steps to the top—there's a little chapel half-way up where one can rest.' He began to point out the various buildings and churches as they drove into the heart of the city, turned off the main road and finally stopped in a quiet street of old houses. There was a canal running down its centre, lined with trees. Louise would have liked to have had the time to gaze but the Daimler was already parked at the edge of the canal and Aldo turned the Rolls into the space beside it.

They crossed the street together and he tugged the old-fashioned bell-pull by the green-painted door with its ornate fanlight. They were admitted at once by a severe-looking man who greeted them solemnly, led them to a small room at one side of the narrow hall, spoke deferentially to Aldo and left them there.

'By the way,' said Aldo, 'our patient is a baroness, but it is quite correct if you address her as *mevrouw*. Here is Litrik.'

The pair of them, being large men, made the room seem very small. Litrik had nodded to her as he'd joined them, but now there was a subtle difference; he and Aldo had slipped into their special medical world and she had become the nurse attending them to carry out their wishes. She sat composedly while they talked, remembering to apologise briefly for not speaking their own language. After ten minutes or so Litrik asked, 'Right, shall we go?' and he opened the door.

Aldo had warned her that his patient might be rude, by no means an understatement, thought Louise, coping with an elderly lady who needed to be coaxed, cajoled and persuaded to do any of the things required of her. But, if the two doctors were impatient or irritated by the constant delays during the examination, they gave no sign. They were rather alike, she reflected, with their calm faces and bland manner which nevertheless got them their own way eventually.

Louise was left presently to assist the lady to dress again and listen to her grumbles while the two men went away to consult with each other. They were a long time, or so it seemed to her, sitting quietly opposite the old martinet, answering in her calm voice the questions which were fired at her.

Finally she was told that the doctors were ready to leave, and she went downstairs to wait in the hall while they had a last word with their patient, and then she went with them into the bright day outside.

Told to do so, she got into the car beside Aldo and sat quietly as he drove through the city's streets, back towards Ziest and beyond.

'You did very well,' he told her. 'The baroness is quite a difficult patient. She is also a very ill woman, as you could see, of course, for yourself. There is nothing much to be done, I'm afraid. But you can see now why I like to have my nurse with me.'

She murmured a reply, wondering what she was supposed to do with the rest of her day and, as if he had read her thoughts, he said, 'Fran wants to show you the house; Litrik and I will be back this evening around tea time, then you and I are going out to dinner.'

She said faintly, 'Oh, are we?' and then quickly, 'Please don't feel that I need entertaining . . .'

'I don't.' She thought that he was amused. 'In any case, I can't remember making any effort to entertain you, Louise.'

A remark which incensed her so much that she said with a snap, 'When is Mrs Pratt coming back?'

'Like you, I can hardly wait for her to return,' he

told her, which left her choking with temper. It took her the rest of the drive to calm down sufficiently to say, 'It is very kind of you to ask me to go out this evening, but I don't think I want to.'

He drew up outside the van Rijgens' house and got out to open her door. 'We shall leave here about six o'clock,' he told her equably, and got in again and drove away without looking round.

'Well,' breathed Louise, serenity gone to the four winds, 'I never did . . .'

She simply had to swallow her feelings then, for Francesca came round the side of the house with the pram. 'I heard you coming,' she said happily. 'Do you feel like a stroll towards the village? I'm dying to hear about your morning.'

It was difficult to be unhappy in Francesca's company, she was so obviously happy herself. Besides, she asked no questions but chatted about her life in Holland and her own hospital days in England. Louise had quite recovered her normally sensible mind by the time the two men returned, so that she was able to greet Aldo with her usual serenity. After tea she changed into the grey crêpe: plain, elegant and dateless; she was heartily sick of it.

In the car driving back towards Utrecht, Aldo observed, 'We are going a few miles the other side of the city to a well-known beauty spot. I hope you will enjoy it.'

'It is nice to have a chance to see something of Holland.' It was a silly remark to make, but somehow the easy formal friendship they'd had had sunk without trace and there was a restraint—that wasn't the right word, she pondered silently; perhaps tension described it better—between them.

She sat silent as they circled round Utrecht and turned away from the motorway to a narrow country road which after a mile or so became well wooded. Presently she could see a river to the right of the road. There were villages at first and then, at intervals, lovely country houses, each set in its own grounds leading down to the river.

'Oh, this is beautiful,' said Louise, 'and so . . . Well, it's like stepping back into a long time ago.'

'Well, in a way it is. These houses were built by rich merchants in the eighteenth and nineteenth centuries; most of them are still privately owned.' They passed an ancient castle as he spoke. 'That is Slot Zylen, still lived in by the family; some very nice Gobelin tapestries are inside.'

'Oh, is it open to the public?'

'Er—yes, I believe so.' He turned the car under a gated arch as he spoke, and along a curving drive with trees and shrubs on either side. It ended in a wide sweep with a large ornamental pond on one side of it and the house on the other. It was a large house, but charming, with a wing jutting out on either side of the main part, forming a three-sided courtyard. The windows were big and latticed, and the roof was really three high gables, each with small dormer windows, exactly spaced. There was a clock high above the door, and it chimed seven o'clock as Louise got out of the car, to stand very quiet, looking up at Aldo with a small frown.

He smiled down at her. 'My home,' he told her. 'Come in and meet my mother and father.'

He took her arm and urged her towards the door,

and as they reached it it was opened by a thin old man with a slight stoop whose face broke into a wide smile as Aldo shook his hand. 'This is Teen,' he told Louise. 'He has been with us since before I was born.'

She shook the old man's hand and returned his smile, and went through the inner door into the hall: wide and square with panelled walls and a vast chandelier. To her slightly fevered fancy there seemed to be massive arched doors whichever way she looked; it was like being plunged into a dream. She allowed her coat to be taken before Aldo put a hand on her arm and led her to one of the doors.

The room beyond was large and lofty and furnished with massive wall cabinets, roomy armchairs and a number of small tables bearing lamps and framed portraits. At one of these tables two people sat playing cards, but they got up as Aldo opened the door and came to meet them.

They were both tall, his mother still pretty with bright blue eyes and fair hair which hardly showed the grey. She was a big woman and elegant, but she was smiling now and cried, 'Aldo, there you are.' She put up her face to be kissed. 'My dear, how lovely to see you.' She turned to Louise. 'And this is Louise.' She took Louise's hand in hers and beamed at her. 'We are so happy to meet you, my dear.'

Aldo had been talking to his father, and Louise thought how alike they were as she shook hands with him and then was borne away to sit on one of the vast sofas beside her hostess where, with a glass of sherry in her hand, she listened to that lady's pleasant chat and tried not to look at Aldo, sitting across the room from her, very much at his ease. But then, why shouldn't he be? He was in his own home.

They dined presently, in a splendid room at a table bright with silver and crystal, and Louise, still bemused, ate *quenelles* of sole, saddle of lamb and a *bavarois* of raspberries without tasting any of them, replying rather shyly to her host's gentle talk and feeling just as shy when Aldo addressed her, for this was an Aldo she didn't know at all.

They sat around over coffee for an hour or so and Louise, allowing herself to drift along in what still seemed a dream, began to enjoy herself. Presently, when they got up to go, she bade her host and hostess goodbye with real regret. They were dears and, as for Aldo, it was like seeing another side of him.

All the same, common sense reasserted itself once they were driving back. 'Why did you invite me to your home?' she asked.

'Now that,' said Aldo, 'is a question I hesitate to answer for the moment.'

'Why?'

'I'll tell you that, too, all in good time.'

She had to be content with that.

CHAPTER NINE

THE PATIENT to be visited on the following day lived on the outskirts of Utrecht, and the consultation had been arranged for two o'clock in the afternoon. Only Francesca was at the table when Lousie went down to breakfast.

'They were away early,' she explained, 'Litrik has a morning round and Aldo went over to Leiden; he's an examiner at the medical school there.'

Louise accepted the coffee and thought that every day revealed something else about Aldo. 'But he works in England,' she said.

'Oh, I know, but he's by way of being international, if you see what I mean, in his particular field. Litrik examines too and has to travel around from time to time.'

'Don't you miss him?'

Francesca laughed. 'No, you see I go, too, so do Nanny and Benedict.'

Louise squashed a feeling of envy. 'Did Aldo leave a message for me? Am I supposed to do anything this morning?'

'Oh, no. Only potter around and have an early lunch. Aldo will pick you up just after one o'clock; his patient is on the other side of Utrecht and he will have to drive right through the city and it's market day. It's a pity you aren't here longer; you must come again with some time to explore.'

Louise agreed that would be nice, but thought it would be unlikely. She looked wistful without knowing it, and Francesca asked, 'Haven't you got a boyfriend, Louise? You are so very pretty and so nice . . .'

Louise went pink. 'No, I haven't. I haven't had much time—to meet people; at hospital all night and my sisters and brother—they are all younger than I am—quite a bit younger.'

'So you feel you must look after them until they are grown up? Before I married Litrik I lived with three aunts, and I honestly thought I'd live with them for ever because they seemed to depend on me for everything. Only Litrik came along and just—just married me and found them a housekeeper. They're perfectly happy and just think if he hadn't come along when he did I might still be there!'

'But even if . . .' began Louise, and started again. 'No one wants to marry me.'

'That's exactly what I thought,' declared Francesca with a wise shake of her mousy head, 'but here I am married to the most marvellous man. Aldo's almost as nice, though, don't you think so?'

'I don't know him very well,' said Louise sedately.

He arrived back a little early, and Francesca, going into the hall to meet him, asked, 'Have you had some lunch?'

He shook his head. 'No time, the exams ran late.'

Tuggs had come into the hall, too, and Francesca said, 'Tuggs, please get some sandwiches and coffee for the doctor—he has got about ten minutes before he has to go off again.'

'No wonder Litrik dotes on you,' observed Aldo as

they walked to the sitting-room. Louise was waiting there and he smiled across at her. 'Ready?' And, when she nodded, 'I won't be a minute; if we are a few minutes late, Litrik will keep our patient happy—he has a nice bedside manner.'

Weaving a slow way through the crowded centre of the city, Aldo said, 'We'll come into Utrecht on Saturday—I dare say you want to buy something for your family, and I must find something for Potts and Mrs Potts.'

'I can buy chocolates in the village,' objected Louise, anxious not to sound eager.

'So you can, but my dear girl, where is your tact? Fran and Litrik cherish their weekends together, we can at least make ourselves scarce for part of the day.'

'Oh, I hadn't thought of that. Perhaps if you would give me a lift . . . I would like to explore a bit as well as look at the shops. I could meet you whenever you are ready to go back.'

'If I didn't know you better than you know yourself, Louise, I might suspect that I was being given the brush-off.' And, at her indignant gasp, 'No, don't worry, you're only anxious to avoid me. Why?'

'Not avoid you,' said Louise calmly, 'only we don't—that is, we don't seem to get on together, I mean—oh, I don't know what I mean, but I daresay you do.'

'Of course I do. The trouble is there is never time to talk about it. Here we are.'

They were in a wide avenue lined with massive houses, built, she judged, around the end of the nineteenth century. She smiled involuntarily when Aldo said, 'Hideous, aren''t they? Let's go in.'

The patient he had been called in to see was, if possible, even more difficult than the old lady had been, but finally Louise got her coat and left the house with the two doctors. As they crossed the pavement to the cars, Aldo said casually, 'Litrik will take you back, Louise, I've a couple of calls to make. Thanks for your assistance.'

She got in beside Litrik and the Rolls-Royce flashed past them. Dying of curiosity, Louise said, 'I didn't know that Aldo had patients here as well as in England.'

'He hasn't,' said Litrik easily. 'He comes over here to lecture and examine and give second opinions; he's going to visit old friends.'

Louise spent the rest of the journey imagining the old friends—amongst them probably some elegant creature ready to fall into his lap when he whistled . . . She chided herself with the thought; Aldo was in love with Zoë, and because she loved him herself she knew quite well that if he loved a girl, he wouldn't be interested in any other woman. He was going to make a perfect—well, almost perfect—husband. She sighed so deeply that Litrik asked kindly, 'Tired? It was a tiresome afternoon, wasn't it?'

Aldo rang up in the early evening; Louise, on her way downstairs heard Francesca talking to him on the phone. 'Of course we don't mind; we'll take care of Louise for you and don't hurry back, Litrik has some work to do after dinner, so he'll be up until all hours.'

Louise went back upstairs and then came down again as Francesca crossed the hall.

'Aldo has just telephoned—he's out to dinner, so there will just be the three of us—you don't mind?'

'Mind? Of course not.' Louise spoke with her usual calm. 'Litrik told me that he had a lot of friends here—well, of course he would, it's his home town, isn't it? He must miss them.'

They had walked into the drawing-room, where Litrik was pouring their drinks. 'Mostly those he grew up with,' observed Litrik. 'He loves his home at Much Hadham and I must say it is a lovely place.'

They settled down to a gentle chat about rural England and the different types of architecture there and in Holland, which took them through dinner. When they had gone back to the drawing-room, they went and strolled in the garden with the dogs until Louise, mindful of Aldo's remark about the van Rijgens' weekends, declared that she was tired and went to bed.

'I thought she might have wanted to stay up until Aldo came back,' said Francesca thoughtfully.

Her husband tucked her hand under his arm as they wandered round the garden. 'Darling, that is just what she didn't want to do. The dear girl is leaning over backwards to give him the impression that she has no interest in him whatsoever.'

'But she has—anyone can see she has. Aldo's not blind . . .'

He turned her round and held her close. 'My darling, don't worry, there will be a happy ending.' He kissed her and she said softly, 'Like us.'

'Like us.'

Louise, in her room, making no attempt to get ready for bed, tried to make sense of her muddled thoughts. When she had heard that Aldo had gone out for the evening, she had instantly jumped to the conclusion that he would be with a girl and that he ought to be with Zoë, mentally at least, but in all honesty she had to admit that it was on her own behalf that she was so put out. The quicker they were back at Much Hadham, the better. She sat for a long time, not even thinking any more until the sound of a car coming up the drive proclaimed the fact that Aldo was back. She went to bed then; her indignation had gone by this time, washed away by a burst of weeping. She was being silly, she told herself firmly. Aldo had every right to go where he liked and with whom he fancied. He might be in love with Zoë but he hadn't actually said so.

The rest of their stay in Holland passed off quietly enough. She busied herslf with Fran and the baby the next day, and on Saturday she was driven to Utrecht and accompanied by Aldo, good-naturedly intent on showing her round the city and taking her to the most suitable shops for her purchases. He took her to lunch, too, at the Café de Paris, which she guessed—quite rightly—to be both fashionable and expensive. He ordered green herring on toast for her to try, and she eyed the raw, salted fish with some doubt, but had to admit once she had eaten it that it was quite nice. The menu was French and she chose Chicken à la King with tiny new potatoes and mange touts, and finished off her lunch with an ice and whipped cream dish which she declared to be delicious.

She finished her shopping after lunch, chocolates for Christine and Mike, a silver bangle for Zoë and more chocolates for Miss Wills and Miss Squires, and when they went to sit in the cloisters between the university and the Cathedral and listen to the carillon. Fifty bells, Aldo told her quietly. As they sat there, he held her hand in his, and just for a moment her doubts and worries evaporated. To sit there for ever, with her hand in his, listening to the lovely sounds, was complete contentment.

He broke into her reverie gently. 'If you have finished your shopping we might drive along the Vecht across the Loosdrechtsche Plassen and then down to the opposite side of the lake.'

'Oh, I would like that.' She withdrew her hand carefully and he didn't try to stop her. 'Only isn't there anything you want to do? I mean, you must have friends and your family . . .'

'I'll see them tomorrow on our way back. Shall we go?'

He hadn't answered the first part of her question, and she didn't like to repeat it.

Their way led past his home but he didn't stop, continuing along the narrow road until he turned off and crossed the head of the lake and drove slowly through Loenan to Loosdrecht, where he stopped at a small waterside café and they had tea. It was a pleasant afternoon with a blue sky even though the wind was chilly and their surroundings were charming, and Louise under the influence of Aldo's imperturbable manner and his gentle flow of talk, relaxed completely. She got back into the car and sat, hardly speaking, as he drove along the road bordering the lake back to Utrecht. She was conscious of disappointment as he went through the city back to the van Rijgens' house, but they had been away for most of the day and she supposed that he would be going out again that evening.

He stopped the car before the house and looked at his

watch. 'We're going out to dinner, you and I,' he told her. 'Is half an hour long enough for you to change?'

'Won't Francesca be hurt? I mean, arranging dinner and so on . . .'

'Oh, I told her we would be out this evening. She thought it a splendid idea.'

Louise still hesitated. 'I haven't got a very grand dress with me.'

He said seriously, 'You always look very nice, Louise. I do wonder why girls worry so much about clothes.'

They went indoors and found the van Rijgens in the nursery with their small son, and presently Louise went to her room and got the grey crêpe dress Christine had made her pack out of the big clothes closet in her room. It was very simple but might pass muster. She showered and changed and put up her hair, then did her face very carefully. The result wasn't exactly breathtaking, but it would do. She went downstairs and found Aldo in one of his beautifully tailored dark grey suits, and blushed a little when he said, 'Quite delightful, Louise. Fran and Litrik are in the drawing-room. Shall we say goodbye?'

The evening turned out to be everything a girl could wish for. The restuarant was no distance from Zeist, but Aldo took a secondary road across heath and woodland until they reached the outside of Amersfoort, when he turned away, criss-crossing the wooded country, not hurrying and carrying on a casual conversation in his most affable manner, so that Louise's uneasiness was stilled. She had no idea why she felt uneasy, but it seemed to her that the doctor was being vague about the future. She had tried, with one or two carefully thought-out questions, to find out about his feelings for Zoë, but somehow he had never given a satisfactory answer. She hadn't been nosy, only given him the opportunity to talk to her if he wanted to. He didn't, that was obvious.

When they reached the restaurant it was quite impossible to be worried about anything. It was very grand and specialised in seafood, its clientèle, from the look of things, was well heeled and well dressed. She was horribly conscious that the grey dress was hardly in the forefront of fashion, but she was too sensible to let that bother her for more than a moment.

Their table was on the far side of the restaurant, and Aldo, behind her, exchanged greetings with any number of people as they followed the waiter, so that when they were seated she observed, 'You must come here often—a lot of people know you.'

'Well, yes, I suppose so. The lobster here is excellent, would you like that? And shall we start off with the *parfait* of chicken livers with truffles and asparagus?'

So he didn't want to talk about himself, thought Louise, and thereafter chatted brightly about everything under the sun except anything to do with him or his family. The excellent wine he had ordered helped, of course; her tongue, usually so well controlled, had everything its own way for once. She was half way through her sweet—a delicious puff pastry case filled with a nut mousse and swimming in some delectable sauce—when the doctor said simply, 'I wish we were alone.'

The wine had indeed gone to her head. She said brightly, 'Oh, you wouldn't want t t—I mean, all these people—and you know a lot of them, and this is such a super restaurant.' She smiled at him, doing her best to look and sound as though she meant every word. 'We wouldn't have anything to talk about,' she went on recklessly. 'We're from different worlds, aren't we? On two different paths, as it were—you are a respected physician and I was the night sister you encountered from time to time.' She paused to take a sip of wine. 'You've been awfully kind to me and I'm very grateful.' Her truant tongue went on. 'But at least it meant that you met Zoë.'

The doctor listened to all this at first with some astonishment and then with well-hidden amusement and some delight. Indeed, he actually signalled the waiter to fill Louise's glass. It was remarkable what a couple of glasses of vintage white Burgundy could achieve.

'Paths quite often meet,' he observed mildly. He sighed a little. 'Tell me, what are you plans for the future?'

'Plans? Oh, well, a job, something I can fit in with looking after the others and Ivy Cottage . . .'

He asked casually, 'Would you not like to see something of the world, even England? After all, you are highly qualified, and there are always jobs for the more senior nurses. Zoë could take over the housekeeping, could she not?'

'She's working full time. Besides . . .' She hesitated, 'Besides, she'll marry before very long, won't she?'

He took his coffee-cup from her. 'Of that I am quite sure.'

Her euphoria melted away, although it was an answer she had expected. 'So you see, I can't go anywhere—not until Christine and Mike are quite grown up.' She spoke in her sensible way and smiled at him, because she loved him very much and she couldn't help herself.

They left the van Rijgens at midday and Louise smilingly agreed that they were bound to meet again, aware that it was most unlikely. Aldo took the narrow road alongside the Vecht and turned in at his parents' gates. They had been expecting them, for coffee was ready for them, and here again Louise murmured suitably when his mother and father both expressed the hope of seeing her again. She would have liked to have done, for she thought they were both delightful; she must remember to tell Zoë how pleasant they were.

Pieter got into the back of the car when they left and when they reached Schipol carried their bags to the desk, bade them goodbye and drove the Rolls away. Louise boarded the plane and sat down beside Aldo, unfidgeting and silent. He had his briefcase with him, and she was sure he would want to immerse himself in its contents.

Which he did, after making sure that she was quite comfortable and had all she needed. Beyond a short break for coffee and sandwiches, he read solidly, making notes from time to time and she sat with the magazines he had bought for her, pretending to read. Something which the doctor's eyes didn't fail to notice.

The Jaguar was there with a man standing beside it when they left Heathrow. The doctor ushered Louise into the front seat, had a brief conversation with the man and got in beside her.

He drove the brief distance to the Excelsior Hotel opposite the airport and parked the car. 'You must be hungry, I know I am.' He glanced at his watch and took her arm. 'Shall we see what there is to eat?'

An unnecessary question to ask of a four-star hotel. They had wild mushroom soup, breast of duck with black cherries and lemon tart, and since Aldo was driving they drank tonic water. They finished their meal with coffee, carrying on a desultory conversation about this and that, easy enough to sustain on the doctor's part but Louise found it difficult. The more she saw of him, the more she longed to let her muddled feelings tumble out and be sorted out by him. It really was becoming very difficult to maintain her normal sensible manner.

They left the hotel presently and the doctor drove round the motorway and turned off towards Much Hadham, to stop outside Ivy Cottage in nice time for tea. He got out and opened Louise's door and then stood quietly while Zoë, Christine and Mike rushed out to embrace her and Dusty pushed his way among them, anxious not to be overlooked. Louise, trying to answer a dozen questions all at once, turned her head in time to see Zoë fling her arms around Aldo's neck and kiss him. Well, she had expected it, hadn't she? She allowed herself to be borne into the cottage where presently Zoë and Aldo joined them.

'I'll get your bag,' said Aldo, and Louise said politely, 'Thank you, and of course you'll stay to tea . . .'

Which he did, making up for her lack of appetite by eating the sandwiches and cake which Christine had made while carrying on a conversation which included everyone. If Louise was a little silent, they put it down to tiredness after the journey, and no one commented upon it. He got up to go presently and they all went with him to the door, where he turned round and looked at Louise standing behind the others.

He said pleasantly, 'Mrs Pratt will be back tomorrow, so there is no need for you to come to work, Louise.'

He got into his car and drove the short distance to his own home, and they shut the door and began to clear away the tea things. Louise went to the kitchen sink and turned on the tap and started the washing up. She felt peculiar, like someone who had had a sharp blow on the head and at the same time she felt sick.

'That's nice,' observed Zoë, picking up a tea towel and starting on the cups and saucers. 'Now you can have a few days at home.'

Louise agreed a little too quickly and turned thankfully to Mike, who was wanting to know if she had brought anything back with her.

It wasn't too difficult to pretend Aldo hadn't said anything of the sort, for the others asked endless questions about her trip to Holland and then told her, blow by blow, just how they had spent the days she had been away. Miss Wills had been marvellous, they assured her, it was like having an aunt or granny about the place, and she liked coming for she wasn't settling down very well with her sister.

They all went to bed presently, and alone in her room, with nothing else to distract her thoughts, Louise lay in bed and worried. She must have been a poor substitute for Mrs Pratt, since Aldo was so anxious to get rid of her. Why hadn't he told her sooner, or at least hinted at it?

Somehow none of that was as bad as the sight of Zoë with her arms round his neck, kissing him. She would have to do something: to stay and see the two of them together was more than she could bear. Later, when she had got back her normal calm, she would be able to cope.

She turned her pillows once more and closed her eyes, only to open them immediately. Perhaps Miss Wills would come back to Ivy Cottage and housekeep, and she would find a job, for a few months at least, away from home. It struck her a little sadly that Mike and Christine were not children any longer and, although they loved her, as long as there was someone to cook for them and remind them about their manners and keep an eye on them, they would be quite happy. Zoë of course, married to Aldo, would be near enough to keep an eye on them . . .

She closed her eyes at last and slept for an hour or two before getting up to cook breakfast and stuff the first of the washing into the machine. She had wept a good deal during the night, and her pretty nose was faintly pink and there were shadows under her eyes, but no one said anything; Mike and Christine were too intent on their breakfast and getting ready for school, and Zoë, after one quick look, broke into a cheerful chatter which filled in the time before she, too, left the house.

Alone, Louise let Dusty into the garden and left the kitchen door open on to the bright morning. She tidied the house, made her bed and washed up; no one would be home until the late afternoon and she would think about supper later on; in the meantime there was the washing. She hung the first lot on the line and stuffed a second batch into the washing machine, and all the while she wondered what Aldo was doing, which reminded her that she would have to look for a job. She sat down at the table and wrote an advertisement for the *Nursing Times* and one for the local paper; even if she put it in at once and had replies by return, it would be ten days or more before references and interviews and all the rest of it were done with. Temporary work, she stressed in the advertisment, for, the moment Zoë told her that she and Aldo were to be married, she would lay her plans for getting away for a time. She wasn't quite happy about that; the right thing would be for her to stay and keep the home together, but her usual calm common sense seemed to have deserted her . . .

She made coffee and left it to cool, forgetting to drink it, and presently fetched in the dry wash and hung out the second lot. She might just as well do something while she tried to decide what was the best thing to do. It would of course be nice if she could just go away, now this minute, as far away from Aldo as possible. She would avoid him at all costs, which shouldn't be difficult, even though he only lived at the other end of the village.

She began to iron Mike's shirts, her plans quite eclipsed by daydreams, so absorbing that she didn't hear the door-knocker, and when she looked up there was Aldo, standing in the kitchen doorway watching her.

'I knocked,' he said quietly, and smiled a little. He looked tired, but at the same time unshakeably calm. 'We have to talk, Louise.'

'I'm busy.' The sight of him standing there had shattered her dreams, and reality held no comfort. 'Another time.'

'Now.' He leaned over the ironing board and unplugged the iron and set it tidily on its stand. 'You've been crying. Why?'

'That is my business.' Then she contradicted herself. 'You have no good reason and no right not to warn me Mrs Pratt was back. If it wasn't for Zoë . . .'

'What has Zoë to do with us?'

'Well, you're—— That is, you and she . . . I thought . . .'

He smiled then. 'Yes, I've been watching you think for quite a time, my darling, and a more muddled lot of ideas I have yet to guess at. Zoë is your sister, and because she is I'm fond of her, just as I'm fond of Christine and Mike and Dusty, because they are part of you, but it is you I love, dear heart. I fell in love with you a long time ago, but I wasn't sure how to make you aware of it—quite unapproachable you were in your cap and apron with your calm efficiency. I had to wait my chance, didn't I? And when it came I took it, and still you didn't see. Zoë did, but she is in love herself with that young George at her office, so perhaps that made her more observant.'

Louise, still entrenched behind the ironing board, had gone a little pale. 'George?' she echoed stupidly.

'George. And having made that quite clear, we can talk about us. Will you marry me, Louise? So many times I have been on the point of asking you, but really, my dear heart, I cannot go on any longer without you.'

Louise came from behind the ironing board and was instantly plucked into his arms. Any sensible thoughts she might have had were fast disappearing in a welter of happiness. She said uncertainly, her head buried against his shoulder. 'The children . . . the house . . . I can't . . .'

He stopped her there by kissing her soundly, and then, just to make sure, kissing her again. 'Miss Wills will be delighted to housekeep here.'

Her voice came muffled. 'How do you know?'

'I've already asked her.'

Louise lifted her head to look at him. 'But the children . . .'

'Oh, they think it's a splendid idea, especially as you'll be living just across the street. Besides, I thought we might find boarding schools for them, they both long to go.'

'They do? I didn't know.'

'My darling, they love you too much to tell you. As for Zoë she has been waiting for this to happen so that she can fall in love without feeling guilty."

Louise gave a sniff. 'I was going away.'

'Were you, my love? What a waste of time that would have been, for I should have had to have gone after you.'

'Oh! Would you really?'

'Yes, even if it had meant tramping round the world until I found you. That brings me back to my first question. Marry me, darling Louise?'

She stretched her arms around his neck. 'Yes, Aldo, my dear; I've been in love with you for quite a time, you know. I think we shall be very happy.'

He kissed her very thoroughly. 'I am quite sure that we shall.' It sounded like a promise, and Louise, looking up into his face, knew that it was.

HARLEQUIN
Romance

Coming Next Month

Available in March wherever paperback books are sold, or through Harlequin Reader Service:

In the U.S.
901 Fuhrmann Blvd.
P.O. Box 1397
Buffalo, N.Y. 14240-1397

In Canada
P.O. Box 603
Fort Erie, Ontario
L2A 5X3

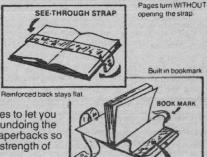

The Pirate
JAYNE ANN KRENTZ

At the heart of every powerful romance story lies a legend. There are many romantic legends and countless modern variations on them, but they all have one thing in common: They are tales of brave, resourceful women who must gentle and tame the powerful, passionate men who are their true mates.

The enormous appeal of Jayne Ann Krentz lies in her ability to create modern-day versions of these classic romantic myths, and her LADIES AND LEGENDS trilogy showcases this talent. Believing that a storyteller who can bring legends to life deserves special attention, Harlequin has chosen the first book of the trilogy—THE PIRATE—to receive our Award of Excellence. Look for it now.

AE-PIR-1A